THE
RIVER
HAS
ROOTS

THE RIVER HAS ROOTS

AMAL EL-MOHTAR

TOR PUBLISHING GROUP
NEW YORK

THE RIVER HAS ROOTS

Copyright © 2025 by Amal El-Mohtar
"John Hollowback and the Witch" © 2023 by Amal El-Mohtar

All rights reserved.

Full-page interior illustrations by Kathleen Neeley
All other interior art by Shutterstock.com

A Tordotcom Book
Published by Tom Doherty Associates / Tor Publishing Group
120 Broadway
New York, NY 10271

www.torpublishinggroup.com

Tor® is a registered trademark of Macmillan Publishing Group, LLC.

The Library of Congress Cataloging-in-Publication Data is available upon request.

ISBN 978-1-250-34108-2 (hardcover)
ISBN 978-1-250-34109-9 (ebook)

Our books may be purchased in bulk for promotional, educational, or business use. Please contact your local bookseller or the Macmillan Corporate and Premium Sales Department at 1-800-221-7945, extension 5442, or by email at MacmillanSpecialMarkets@macmillan.com.

First Edition: 2025

Printed in the United States of America

0 9 8 7 6 5 4 3 2 1

For Hoda Nassim,
who taught me to play,
and for my sister Dounya,
who taught me to sing.

(What is a river but an open throat; what is water but a voice?)

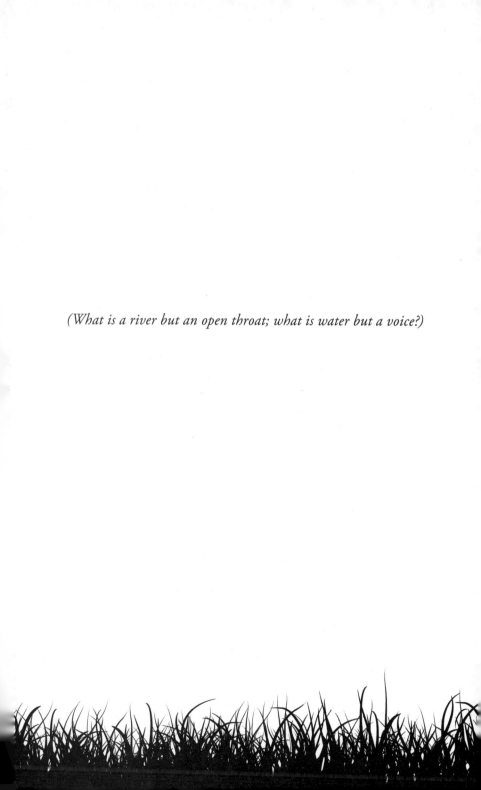

THE
RIVER
HAS
ROOTS

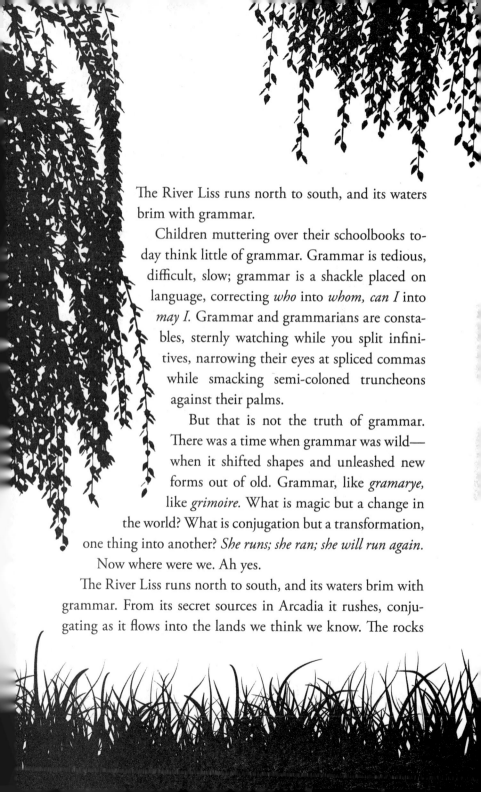

The River Liss runs north to south, and its waters brim with grammar.

Children muttering over their schoolbooks today think little of grammar. Grammar is tedious, difficult, slow; grammar is a shackle placed on language, correcting *who* into *whom, can I* into *may I.* Grammar and grammarians are constables, sternly watching while you split infinitives, narrowing their eyes at spliced commas while smacking semi-coloned truncheons against their palms.

But that is not the truth of grammar. There was a time when grammar was wild— when it shifted shapes and unleashed new forms out of old. Grammar, like *gramarye*, like *grimoire.* What is magic but a change in the world? What is conjugation but a transformation, one thing into another? *She runs; she ran; she will run again.* Now where were we. Ah yes.

The River Liss runs north to south, and its waters brim with grammar. From its secret sources in Arcadia it rushes, conjugating as it flows into the lands we think we know. The rocks over which it tumbles shiver into jewels of many colours. Along its banks nod flowers and grasses, but out of all season or sense: spring bluebells mix with autumn asters, and towering cattails scatter frosted seeds over beds of blooming marigolds. Sometimes the river bends like an elbow, and sometimes it stretches broad and straight as a shadow. So long as you can hear the waters, everything seems possible: that the sun is the moon, that a star is a cloud, that dusk is dawn, and everything is both hallowed and haunted at the same time.

Until, that is, the river meets the willows.

Two tremendous trees, taller and thicker than any willow you've ever seen, stand on either side of the River Liss, and they bend towards each other like dancers, or lovers, reaching out to clasp each other. Their roots knobble the water's surface from beneath, twist together into a braided sort of bridge; their branches above tangle and pleach into a vast, vaulting canopy.

Willows are great grammarians. Their roots are uncommon thirsty; like tightly woven nets they sift gram after gram of bucking wildness from the water and pull it into their bodies. The river may conjugate everything it touches, but the willows translate its grammar into their growth, and hold it slow and steady in their bark.

South of those two great trees—let us call them, as the common folk do, the Professors—the landscape stills and settles. Seasons know their place. A long procession of willows, diminishing in size and strangeness, lines the banks of the River Liss in even, coppiced stitches, so that by the time the Liss reaches the western edge of the bustling town of Thistleford, its waters are quite tame.

But if you were to stand and behold those first two trees—if you were a stranger to the land, and unaccustomed to the sight—you might hear a kind of hum in the air, or feel it as a thickness in your chest. You might think that something about the shape of those trunks, the sweep of their twisted crowns, reminds you of something, or someone, you've lost—something, or someone, you would break the world to have again. *Something, you might think, happened here, long, long ago; something, you might think, is on the cusp of happening again.*

But that is the nature of grammar—it is always tense, like an instrument, aching for release, longing to transform present into past into future, *is* into *was* into *will.*

At the time of our story the willows of the River Liss belonged mostly to the Hawthorn family, whose holdings hugged both sides of the river's length from Thistleford to the Modal Lands out past the Professors' roots. Those shifting, shimmering lands stopped at an assemblage of standing stones folk called the Refrain; beyond it was Faerie, and everyone knew it, even if no one spoke in words so plain. No one looks directly at the sun, for all it illuminates the world, and Faerie being the source of so much grammar made folk apt to speak of it in a kind of translation. They called it Arcadia, the Beautiful Country, the Land Beyond, Antiquity. And if they sometimes meant things less pretty than those names suggested, well, there are always things lost in translation, and curious things gained.

Despite their name, the Hawthorn family's work was willows, and had been for as long as anyone alive could remember. They tended, they planted, they coppiced and harvested the trees, making good use of every part: the leaves for tea, the bark for medicines

and baskets and cordage, the wood for furniture
and instruments. Grammarians wanted the wood for
their wands, and the common folk wanted it for its more
passive enchanted properties: a willow flute might lead rats
from a barn, while a willow bed might ease the weary into lucid
dreams.

But a foolhardy few, armed with willow-bark nets and shallow baskets of tight willow weave, crept carefully beyond the Professors' roots to pan for raw, unfiltered grammar. Carefully they combed the water to catch at small, thick chunks of enchantment, taking great pains not to wet their own skin. If they caught so much as a single undissolved gram, they could make a small fortune—even after subtracting the king's duties in Thistleford—by selling them to grammarians for conjugation. Grammarians tended to clump together like clauses at the universities of the east and north, breaking language into their meanings, and received grammar for their projects only once it had been refined and made regular; few ventured into Grammarye towns, and then only grudgingly, like potters with a disdain for mud. Middlemen thrived in the trade.

You might well ask, why would these prospective gram catchers be so few? Why didn't every latecomer rush out beyond the Professors' trunks to drag baskets through the wild waters of the Liss for a chance at great fortune?

And you might find, after asking, that the Modal Lands between the Professors and the Refrain were peculiarly thick with strange wildlife. You might find your attention caught by small grey rabbits with uncommonly human eyes; you might see your name spelled out by a clump of nettles waving in the wind; you might feel a deep ache in your breast while hearing a bird singing with a dolorously human voice, the pain of which no one, not even the willows, could translate away.

Marred is what people called the unwelcome actions of grammar, and like paper torn by the press of a pencil, there was no way to set them right.

What the town of Thistleford gained from its proximity to Faerie was obvious: prosperity, merriment, uncommonly good weather. What it lost was negligible—the cost of doing business.

But we were speaking of the Hawthorn family, weren't we, and their willow work—their coppicing, their basket-weaving, their management of this enchanted resource. Here is a secret that isn't, really, for everyone knew it even if they didn't understand the custom: the Hawthorn family's true work was to *sing* to the willows. By ancient treaty this was only required four times a year, at the turning of the seasons; by long-standing tradition, it was done every day, at sunrise and sunset, the way one bids one's family members good morning on waking and good night before bed. Just as beekeepers tell their hives all the news in thanks for honey, the Hawthorns sang to their trees in thanks for their translations. But none had ever taken to the task quite so vigorously as Esther and Ysabel Hawthorn, the latest daughters of that house.

When people say that voices run in families, they mean it as inheritance—that something special has been passed down the generations, like the slope of a nose or the set of a jaw. But Esther and Ysabel Hawthorn had voices that ran together like raindrops on a windowpane. Their voices threaded through each other like the warp and weft of fine cloth, and when the sisters harmonized, the air shimmered with it. Folk said that when they sang together, you could feel grammar in the air. If they sang a stormy sky, the day clouded over. If they sang adventure, blood rose to the boil. If they sang a sweet sadness, everything looked a little silver from the corners of the eyes.

Esther was two years the elder, with hair dark as the December of her birth, and if this story were a folk tale or an old song, she'd be certain to have a disposition as frosty; Ysabel was the younger, and because her own hair was bright as kings' coins or summer corn, you might think she was given to chatter and merriment. But this was not the truth of them, singly or together. Esther was thoughtful and gregarious, and while Ysabel had a laugh loud and easy as barrel-tumbled apples in the fall, she was in fact very shy.

They loved each other utterly, and everyone in Thistleford knew it.

Though their voices had the sheen of grammar, Esther and Ysabel were not themselves grammarians, and in truth, they felt nothing especially uncanny about their home. The silver-green of willow leaves was familiar comfort to them, and the sisters read their moods like weather. The willows themselves felt like ancestry, like kin. They cherished the Professors in particular, for their height and their shade and the sound of the wind rustling through their leaves like chimes—but they loved even more the stories told of them, of how the Professors came to bow their leafy heads together over the River Liss. Their father told them that the Professors loved each other in a forbidden love, and they were driven from their homes into the river, and conjugated into trees; their mother said they'd made some great sacrifice for the good of their families, given themselves to the river in exchange for a secret gift. But whatever details blurred and shifted in the telling, the fact that the Professors had been and still were lovers never came into dispute; they had *professed* their love, hence the name.

From their earliest days, Esther and Ysabel never shirked their duty, singing the required hymn with great solemnity at the changing of every season. Strange to tell, it wasn't in English; they couldn't say what language it was, only that the shape of the words fit so differently into their mouths that they felt their voices shift in deference to it. Their mother told them that *her* parents had thought it was Welsh, until the day a Levantine woodworker staying with the family had said it sounded to her like Arabic, but a dialect she'd never heard. Either it was older than her, or from a place she'd never travelled ("or," their mother said, ruefully, "my accent was too atrocious to understand and she was too polite to say so").

But the woodworker had been able to explain some of it; it was, their mother told them, a song about the North Wind opening doors and carrying messages to and from a beloved in exile. So the girls knew it as the Professors' Hymn, and though they didn't really understand it—they argued, sometimes, about whether the North Wind *was* one of the lovers, or merely a messenger—they enjoyed improvising harmonies into the repetition of nonsense *la* sounds in the long refrain, inflecting it slightly differently depending on the time of year, and how likely the North Wind was to blow.

As Esther and Ysabel grew, as singing became their favourite pastime, they began to play with adding new material to their repertoire. It did the trees no harm, and seemed even to do them

some good; their parents observed small shifts of
colour in bark and leaf, though any other effects
were too subtle to track without a grammarian. But if any
grammarian would stoop to such common work, instead
of the fire and crackle of conjugation in the king's service, they
hadn't yet wandered towards Thistleford. Or if they had—and
only one had—they tended towards Arcadia, and never came
out again.

Taste is a kind of language, and siblings speak it with a forked
tongue. As entwined as Esther and Ysabel were, there came a
point in their childhood where their interests diverged, and, like
the Professors, they loved each other across the gap between
them. Ysabel loved pickles where Esther couldn't abide the smell
of vinegar; Esther took to foraging while Ysabel preferred gardening; Ysabel was fascinated by boys and their company while
Esther found them tedious and enjoyed being alone.

Where music was concerned, Ysabel loved flutes and murder
ballads best, while Esther favoured harps and riddle songs. They
often teased each other over their favourites, argued over what
kind of music the willows preferred while gathering branches or
stripping bark.

"All I'm saying," mused Ysabel, bundling long strips of bark
together into tight coils, "is that if I had died for love, I'd like to
hear William and Margaret songs best. Songs of love winning
out, of holding each other forever, even at the bottom of a river."

Esther was weaving a basket, but paused in her work to look
up and squint at her sister in amusement. "Bel, really? Do you
love murder ballads because you want to be murdered? Or be-

cause you don't, not really, but you get to have it safely in six stanzas and a looping refrain?"

Ysabel laughed. "You've turned it backwards! I'm saying if I *were* murdered, the ghost of me might still like to hear murder ballads!"

"Or," said Esther, "you might go off them completely. I'd certainly find them less thrilling from the receiving end of a penknife."

Ysabel rolled her eyes. "Fine, fine. What do *you* think they like best?"

Esther looked at the trees thoughtfully. "Travelling songs, like their hymn. Sea songs. Songs that bring news from away."

"So, Miss Hawthorn," Ysabel said, raising an eyebrow and deepening her voice into a pitch-perfect mimicry of an insufferable headmaster from their school days, "it is your contention that people must in fact most ardently desire that which they cannot have? You don't think that songs of travel are liable to sadden those rooted into the earth? Besides"—she smiled, reaching up to touch one's trunk—"surely the river brings them all the news worth telling."

"Only from one direction," said Esther, watching the water flow. "That's just it; I think they'd welcome news of mortal lands, mortal work. And there's no singing in Arcadia."

Ysabel went quiet for a moment, then worked her fingers into the grass. Too lightly, she said, "Did Rin tell you that?"

Esther nodded, then bent her gaze back to her weaving. Ysabel waited for more, but her sister stayed quiet, so she shrugged.

"Well, Rin's wrong. *We* sang in Arcadia, when we were lost."

Esther paused, again, and looked at Ysabel; it was so rare that she mentioned it.

"But we're not Arcadian. It's not that it's forbidden," she said, carefully. "Arcadians just . . . don't.
Or can't. They play instruments, but they never sing. And
if I were ever to live there, Rin said I'd eventually forget
how."

"But," said Ysabel, "you said Rin loves your singing."

Esther looked back to her weaving, nodded. "They do."

Ysabel narrowed her eyes, reached for her sister's hand, and
twined their fingers together tightly. "Well. Rin can think what
they like. If you were ever in danger of forgetting how to sing, I
would simply have to come and remind you."

Esther chuckled, but Ysabel went on, teasing. "Every other
week. You'll come here, then I'll go there, and there won't be a
week we don't see each other, and sing together. I don't care how
golden and honeyed Arcadia is, I won't let you forget a single
word of 'Tam Lin.'"

"Ugh," laughed Esther. "Mercy! That tedious tune! We always leave off a few verses!"

"We won't anymore! In fact, we'll invent new ones! I'll make
you learn them!"

"Fine, fine," said Esther, reaching out to pet her sister's hair.
"Thank you, Bel. I accept your proposed tyrannies. And anyway,"
she said, aiming for lightness and missing it with a thud, "you
know—you do know I would never leave you for Arcadia."

Ysabel smiled like a page turning. "What shall we sing to
the trees?"

They settled on "The Dowie Dens of Yarrow," and if the willows bent their branches towards them as they sang, trailed them
even lower into the water, the sisters never noticed.

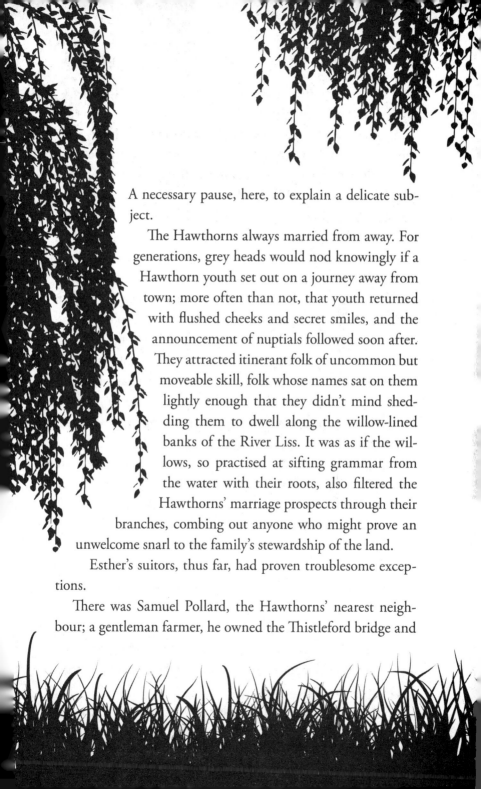

A necessary pause, here, to explain a delicate subject.

The Hawthorns always married from away. For generations, grey heads would nod knowingly if a Hawthorn youth set out on a journey away from town; more often than not, that youth returned with flushed cheeks and secret smiles, and the announcement of nuptials followed soon after. They attracted itinerant folk of uncommon but moveable skill, folk whose names sat on them lightly enough that they didn't mind shedding them to dwell along the willow-lined banks of the River Liss. It was as if the willows, so practised at sifting grammar from the water with their roots, also filtered the Hawthorns' marriage prospects through their branches, combing out anyone who might prove an unwelcome snarl to the family's stewardship of the land.

Esther's suitors, thus far, had proven troublesome exceptions.

There was Samuel Pollard, the Hawthorns' nearest neighbour; a gentleman farmer, he owned the Thistleford bridge and

several fields downriver from the Hawthorns' willow stands. A union between their families would
bring about a union of their lands, and draw the Hawthorns closer to the wholesome, settled tameness of Thistleford. This in and of itself was not so terrible—except that Esther
could not bear Samuel Pollard's company. His eyes always had
the soft, beseeching expression of a whining dog; his hands,
bafflingly, were always somehow both cold and moist, and he
was forever finding ways to accidentally brush Esther's skin with
them. He had gone to one of the great universities—Esther refused to remember which—and returned speaking both Latin
and poetry, which he saw fit to share as often as he could though
he plainly spoke neither very well. He thought himself gal-
lant—he aspired to gallantry—and he often brought Esther and
Ysabel little gifts from his trips to London and Exeter, hinting of
his political prospects to their bemused parents. Esther regarded
him with that species of contempt bred by long familiarity and
short temper.

(To Esther's baffled irritation, Ysabel said she liked the man,
saw nothing objectionable about him, and even claimed to admire his verse—though Ysabel, it must be said, was not usually
the one bearing the full brunt of his recitations.)

But then there was Rin.

Rin came from Arcadia. Rin had a name that Esther could
not hold wholly in her head, though they'd whispered it to her
once, and when they did, what she grasped in images and feelings was *glint of frost on the long grasses in a winter dawn.* Rin was
a feeling, a lightness in her step, a burr in her throat; some days
she thought she'd made them up inside her head, so difficult was
it to put words to them.

She had told no one but Ysabel about her lover—though

people talked, of course, towns being what they are, and the Hawthorns being of such uncommon interest to them all.

Esther didn't know what to do with Rin. She knew what she wanted to do—she knew this with great enthusiasm and precision—but she couldn't grasp a future with them any more than she could grasp the river water in her bare hands. Arcadians were only about as novel in the area as any other foreigners, but they tended to visit, not stay; trysts were not uncommon, but marriages were. People sometimes fell into or out of Arcadia by accident—Esther and Ysabel had as children—but no one who'd set out on purpose to travel there had ever returned, and opinion was divided on whether that was because Arcadia was too delightful to leave or too dangerous to survive.

(There was of course the most obvious answer, which most folk didn't discuss: that a traveller might emerge from Arcadia a hundred years after having ventured in, however little time they'd spent within its borders. But no one in Thistleford could remember it happening; perhaps it merely hadn't happened yet.)

Everything was riddles with Rin, and as much as Esther loved riddles, her chief pleasure was in solving them. Pollard was a loose thread begging to be pulled; Rin was a knot that would not come undone.

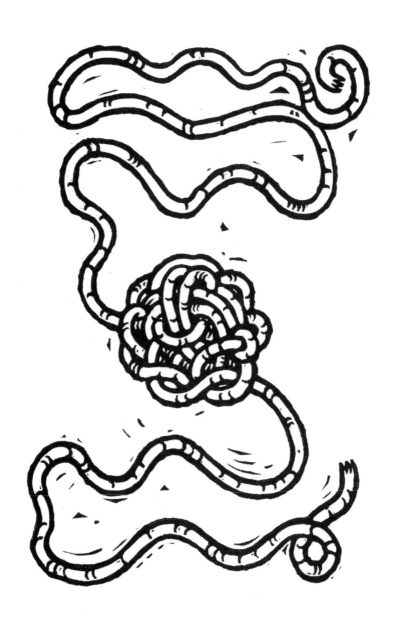

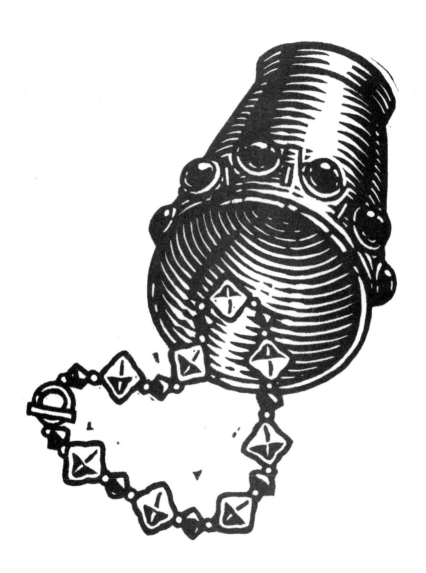

The first time Esther met Rin, they were a storm. While walking in the Modal Lands she was caught in a howling gale, and took shelter beneath one of the granite outcroppings that littered the area near the Refrain. There was a great clashing in the air, and the sort of mixing weather common to the borders of Arcadia, a swirl of hail and thunder. It was so loud and dreadful that Esther began singing to drown it out—"The False Knight on the Road," a riddle song with a tune somewhere between jaunty and mournful, just as she liked them.

By the end of the first verse the hail melted to heavy rain. By the end of the second verse the rain began to taper off. By the end of the third verse the storm fell away like an unclasped cloak, and late afternoon light glistened on the wet granite like grammar.

She finished the song—it always felt wrong to begin a song without ending it—and stepped out from beneath the shelter. A silver bracelet, delicately etched with stars, glinted in the grass at her feet.

But people sometimes left offerings in the Modal Lands, and Esther had been taught from her earliest childhood not to disturb them; it wouldn't do to pick up other folks' hopes and dreams, however accidentally. So she stepped lightly around the bracelet and went home.

The second time Esther met Rin, they were a snowy owl, incongruously bright in the bare branches of a wintering tree, tearing into a vole. Esther had stepped into the Modal Lands to gather bowls of snow; it was high summer in Thistleford, and she wanted to drizzle them with honey for a treat. But the owl looked so rare and strange and bloody that she found herself singing "Childe Owlet" to it, one of Ysabel's more gruesome favourites, before she quite realized what she was doing.

The owl stopped eating. It swayed, slightly, as she sang. When she finished, the owl flew away, and she turned to go home, but heard a clang of metal on stone behind her.

On a flat rock by the river, a jewelled cup lay toppled on its side, spilling out a silver bracelet etched with stars.

Esther crouched down to examine them. She began to feel the grammar of a story circling her, the grammar of *two out of three*.

She left the cup and the bracelet, filled her bowls with snow, and returned to her family.

The third time Esther met Rin, they were a woman playing a harp. The moon was full in the Modal Lands, and the wind was blowing from the north, carrying the sound of harp strings to Thistleford. But no one heard them but Esther, who rose from her bed and wandered from the house; on bare feet she stepped carefully past the Professors' roots, and stopped at what she saw there.

They had long white hair, tied back in black ribbon. They

wore a green shirt with billowing sleeves, cuffed tightly at the wrist, and a black skirt embroidered along the waist and hem in silver, catching the moonlight. Their hands were pale and moved over the strings like they were shaping a story from them.

They stopped playing when Esther saw them, and looked at her across the span of the River Liss.

"Why won't you let me requite you?" they said.

Their voice made Esther think of weather, of winter, of wood-smoke: something cold but bright, burning and fragrant, curling into the air before vanishing. They were utterly strange and utterly beautiful, in a way that Esther yearned towards because she didn't understand it, the way she yearned towards horizons and untrodden secret paths in unfamiliar woods.

It took her a moment to focus on their words, and another moment to reply,

"Requite me for what?"

"Your songs," they said. "You gave them to me, and I must pay you for them. But you keep refusing."

Esther shook her head. "They cost me nothing to give. I sang to please myself."

The harper closed their eyes. "O what is crueller than the frost," they murmured, running their thumb over the strings, "a gift far greater than its cost."

Esther's eyes shone. She'd never heard that one.

The harper went on, "I can hear them, still—'The False Knight,' the 'Owlet Childe.' I treasure them. You must have something from me, if I am to keep them."

Esther frowned. "I don't understand. You're a musician—can you not remember the tunes? They're both rather common—"

The harper looked at her as if she'd grown another head.

"Your singing," they said, gently, "is not . . . common.
I want—" they said, and it seemed to Esther that something
in their voice was stiffening, deepening around an unspeakable
ache, "to recall the songs as you sang them."

Esther felt very stupid as she said, "Would you like me to
sing them to you again?"

The harper looked away with so much anguish that Esther
felt herself sinking into nightmare. This was a riddle, a real one,
come to her from Arcadia, and here she was failing to solve it.

The harper suddenly stood, and placed a hand on the harp's
neck.

"I brought you this," they said, and now their voice made
Esther think of a well at night, dark and echoing the sound of
coins thrown into it. "It is my most prized possession. I shaped
it from the space between seven stars and strung it with silk
spun from their light. I beg of you not to refuse it, nor to sing to
me again until we've reached an agreement."

Esther stared at the harp—sleek and black as an otter swim-
ming, white strings that shimmered with grammar. She thought
about gifts, and Samuel Pollard, and how much she hated him
giving her things she hadn't asked for—tortoise-shell combs,
lengths of fancy ribbon—under the guise of being neighbourly
when they were clearly meant for courting. She thought about
how the gift forced a bond on her that was awkward and difficult to refuse, and how payment could dispel that, could break
the bond.

There was a grammar, too, to gifts.

The harper, she thought, was asking her to release them from
something—but saying that they did, also, *want* what she'd

unwittingly given. That it was too much to carry without balancing the exchange.

And Esther did not want this to be the last time they met.

"I have a bargain for you," said Esther, "if you'll take it. I've long wanted to play the harp—would you teach me?"

"Yes," they said, immediately, and then sank to their stone seat again, and closed their eyes. All the glittering ice of them softened; they all but melted the harp back against their shoulder (Esther, inexplicably, blushed) and raised their hands to the strings. All of a sudden they were playing "The False Knight on the Road" as if it were accompanying a voice, and in another moment had blended it into "Childe Owlet," then back out again.

Esther watched, and listened, and felt her heart twist inside her.

"Thank you," they said, when they'd finished. They looked peaceful, now. "Thank you. You may call me Rin."

"Rin," she said. "I'm Esther, by the way."

"I know," they said. When Esther blinked, they said, "There is a witch who runs a mill in Arcadia—"

"Not Agnes Crow?" said Esther, softly, wondering.

"She is a neighbour," they said. "I asked her counsel in how to approach you. She suggested"—they gestured at themselves—"wearing a shape that could talk to you."

"Sound advice," said Esther, looking towards the Refrain. "My sister and I gave her a chicken once, and she showed us the way out of Arcadia. But it was a long time ago."

Rin looked at Esther closely, with a kind of gentle scrutiny that made her feel like there was a brush running through her hair.

"I see it on you. That you've been in Arcadia. That it left a mark on you."

"I see," said Esther, with a boldness she would later marvel at for days, "that we have many things we could share with each other, if you're interested in further trade. Perhaps someday you'll give me something worth another song."

She couldn't put words to the look on Rin's face. She only knew, very sharply and deeply, that she wanted to go on being the cause of it.

MILWICH
EGGS & LOAVES.

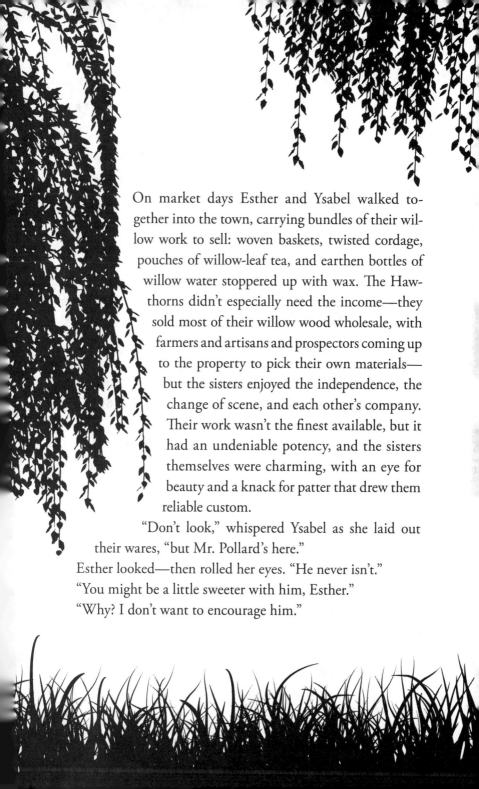

On market days Esther and Ysabel walked together into the town, carrying bundles of their willow work to sell: woven baskets, twisted cordage, pouches of willow-leaf tea, and earthen bottles of willow water stoppered up with wax. The Hawthorns didn't especially need the income—they sold most of their willow wood wholesale, with farmers and artisans and prospectors coming up to the property to pick their own materials— but the sisters enjoyed the independence, the change of scene, and each other's company. Their work wasn't the finest available, but it had an undeniable potency, and the sisters themselves were charming, with an eye for beauty and a knack for patter that drew them reliable custom.

"Don't look," whispered Ysabel as she laid out their wares, "but Mr. Pollard's here."

Esther looked—then rolled her eyes. "He never isn't."

"You might be a little sweeter with him, Esther."

"Why? I don't want to encourage him."

"That's exactly why," insisted Ysabel. "He's still our neighbour, we'll have to live with—Mr. Pollard! Good morning!"

Tall, spindly, insufferable Mr. Pollard. He approached them, beaming as though Esther had never made plain her dislike of him. Esther ground her teeth; Ysabel winced.

"Good morning, dear ladies," he said, inclining his head towards them with flawless courtesy. "May I assist you in any way?"

Ysabel opened her mouth to speak, but Esther cut in. "That's very kind, but we're all right, thank you. Just about set up."

"Ah," said Pollard, "in that case, could I trouble you for some of your willow water and a basket to carry it in?"

Esther smiled briskly, picked up as many jars of willow water as would fit inside their largest basket, and handed it over to Ysabel to pretty up with flowers and ribbon. "Will this do?"

Pollard raised an eyebrow. "Certainly—"

"Good. It's free of charge, a gift from our family to yours. Now, if you'll excuse us—"

"Esther," said Pollard, leaning in slightly, eyes wide and fervent, "you and I have things we ought to discuss. If you'd consent to walk around the market with me—"

"We have nothing to discuss, Mr. Pollard," said Esther, stiffly.

"Miss Hawthorn," he said, accepting the rebuke but still keeping his voice quiet, "I wish with all my heart to persuade you otherwise. Please. I know you've little interest in me personally, but I would take it as a great kindness if you would allow me to make my case before rejecting it completely."

Esther's cheeks burned.

"Very well," she murmured. "If you meet us here at the end of the day, you can walk us home."

He smiled, a relieved, dimpled affair. "Wonderful. I'll see you then."

He turned to go, but Ysabel called out, "Wait, Mr. Pollard!" and held out his basket, its handle now fetchingly twisted with flowers.

Pollard smiled vaguely, said, "I'll pick it up this afternoon," and wandered off. Ysabel chewed her lip, and set it down. Esther stared at her.

"Ysabel," she said quietly, "do you . . . fancy that man?"

She shrugged. "He's not so bad."

"Bel, he's like a bit of bread that's been dropped in a pond! If the bread could also beg a duck to eat him!"

"Quack, quack," said Ysabel, quirking her lips.

"You're *not* serious!"

"I don't know, Esther," she said, shrugging. "He's only ever been kind to us. And I know you hate his poems, but I think it might be nice, you know. To have someone write poems about me. To be . . . seen, I suppose, like that. Like an angel, or a queen."

There are a great many songs written about sisters, and a great many stories, too, and most often they turn on jealousy, on pettiness, on spite. Just as often as there are cruel stepmothers in ballads there are older sisters jealous of the younger, coveting their looks, their lands, their lovers.

Esther looked at her sister—her beautiful, brilliant sister, talented and generous and funny and kind—and felt her fingers curling into fists at the thought that all the summer sunshine of her could dim for want of being seen by the likes of Samuel Pollard.

"Bel," she said helplessly, around the fire in her throat. "Queen of ducks and angels. You shall have poems written to you with a quill on fire. You shall have songs sung to you by enchanted harps.

Whole branches of grammar will be invented only
to praise you."

Ysabel chuckled, but shook her head. Esther put her
hands on her shoulders and bent their foreheads together.

"Ysabel Hawthorn," she said, and she could not keep the
heat from her voice, "demand better than to be worshipped by
a *crumb*."

Her sister laughed, then, a real laugh, and Esther smiled and
swallowed the coals she longed to heap on Pollard's oily head.

Although they had sensibly packed a lunch, around noon Ysabel
sent Esther away from the stall to find them some treats, "because," she said, "you're *still scowling* even if you don't think you
are and people are scared to come and chat," so Esther rolled her
eyes and went for a stroll around the square.

She did enjoy market days; in addition to the food stalls selling fruit, meat, milk, and cheese, there were woollens and instruments, toys and pottery, candles and soap. She liked seeing people
hawking—her neighbours transformed as by a stage, putting on
the self that sold vegetables like a mummer's mask, their voices
brighter and bolder, their eyes more twinkling. It was exhaust-
ing, too—the arguing back and forth, everyone angling for a
bargain—but the bustle of it once in a while was a pleasant exer-
tion, a glimpse into something more than real, a stirring up of the
mundane into grammar. Things could *happen* on market days.

She felt a tug at her sleeve.

She turned, and saw a small child blink wide brown eyes at
her, press some crumpled paper into her palm, and run away.
She smoothed it open; it was a woodcut advertisement for Mil-

wich Eggs and Loaves, and featured a chicken foregrounded against a small mill.

Rin. They were here, somewhere, for all they hated crowds—in some mortal seeming she hadn't yet met. Their meetings in the Modal Lands had grown less frequent, of late; Rin had explained that it was difficult to keep appointments outside of Arcadia without some debt calling to them. The day that Esther felt, in her heart, that she'd learned to play the harp, that debt no longer anchored them; but if she stood near the Refrain and sang, they often appeared within the hour, if they weren't otherwise engaged. It was a strange way of courting—nothing Esther had been raised to expect. It was crushing, too, to sing to the evening and receive nothing in the way of reply.

She looked around for someone selling eggs.

Of the three people doing so, she knew two: Nancy Abbot, gruff as her infamous billy goats, and Giles Hogg, a twinkle-eyed duffer who flirted with everyone who approached. The third wore a grey smock over muddy trousers and a wide-brimmed straw hat despite sitting in the shade, and smiled when Esther began making her way over in a slow, diffident meander.

She leaned over the crates without looking at the person selling them, and picked up an egg.

"Friend," she said, quietly, "have you travelled far today?"

This was the traditional way to address one who might have come by the Antique Lands. It was sometimes a gamble; folk who knew the custom took offense at being so mistaken, and locals sometimes said it in jests of varying cruelty when one's behaviour was at odds with Thistleford norms.

Though there was only one question, there were many replies, and the egg vendor inclined their head and gave one of them.

"I've travelled light, I've travelled dark, and I'm still on my way," they said quietly. Their features were unfamiliar—their eyes rounder, their lips fuller, their hair short and brown and curly where Esther was accustomed to seeing it long and straight and white—but Rin's voice, indescribably changeable as it was, remained always and only theirs.

Esther smiled, and put the egg back in place. "I didn't expect to find you here. Are these from Agnes?"

Rin nodded. "She required me to tell you that these are Kitty Grey's finest yet."

"*Still?* It's been thirteen years, how . . ." She shook her head. "Grammar."

"I don't think it is grammar; I think she's just happy there. Agnes' daughter has a way with her. And there's the open question of time, of course. But Agnes asked me to pass on her regards, three dozen eggs, and requests, let me see"—they reached into a pocket and pulled out a folded piece of paper, flecked here and there with petals from unfamiliar flowers—"willow water, a pouch of your tea blend, and, if possible, for you and Ysabel to sing the following songs to the Professors during the first quarter of the next moon."

Esther took it, and read down the list. "Did she say why?"

"I did not ask, but I presume it's to do with her research."

Esther folded the paper back up and slipped it into her own pocket. "I wish she'd come back, just for a little, and explain it to me."

"I rather suspect that would upset her research. But I have another note for you, if you'll take it," said Rin, and handed her something so delicately and intricately folded that it was very nearly a circle. "But don't open it here. I should be on my way—I have some other errands to run while I'm on this side of the border. I'll make sure the eggs arrive on your parents' doorstep before you're home."

This did not mean, Esther knew, that Rin would deliver them personally, or in a recognisable shape; they had some deep-seated and very foreign sense of propriety about when it was correct to meet a lover's family. But living so near the Refrain, the Hawthorns had become accustomed, over generations, to having parcels delivered to them by deer, foxes, badgers, and the occasional wood pigeon or crow; her parents would not be unnerved by the arrival of three dozen eggs the day after their last hen stopped laying. They would simply step outside and thank the Professors.

Esther pocketed the note and said, "I could send Ysabel over with the willow water and tea."

It hung in the air for a moment.

Then Rin said, gently, "I do not think it is time."

"She already knows about you—"

"Esther—"

"She keeps wondering if she's *already* met you—"

"Esther," said Rin, more firmly, "she has not."

She sighed. "Send a runner over, then." She looked at Rin—infuriating, always beautiful no matter the seeming they wore—and closed her fist over the paper in her pocket, hoping for a promise.

Esther came back to their stall with a punnet of blackberries and a mood to match. Ysabel took one look at her sister and stage-whispered, "Are *they* here?" She craned her neck around while Esther chuckled. "Can I meet them this time?"

"No," she said, and Ysabel's face fell. Esther fished around in her pocket for Agnes' note. "But Agnes Crow sent us some eggs, a shopping list, and asked us to sing these songs."

Ysabel took the paper. "Hm," she said, puzzled, "I don't know this one."

"Which one? I thought they were all in our repertoire."

Ysabel read:

> When the moon is on the wane,
> Read the wood against its grain.
> Sing no song and forge no chain.
> Do not seek me out; Refrain.

Esther squeaked and snatched the note back, then went pink from chin to cheek while Ysabel laughed. "So you do like it when *some* folk write you poetry!"

"It is *not* poetry," said Esther, attempting to recover some dignity, "it's a *riddle,* which is completely different."

"Mm," said Ysabel, who could waggle her eyebrows with devastating timing and precision. "Obviously. So did you quarrel? Why don't they want to see you?"

Esther blushed deeper. "No, they—they do. See, the moon is waning right now, so . . . You have to read the rest as its opposite. They want me to meet them at the Refrain tonight."

"I see," said Ysabel, grinning. "So the part about *not* singing and *not* . . . forging . . . Esther Hawthorn, what *do* you two get up to out there?"

"I'll explain when you're older!"

When Rin's runner came to pick up the goods, they were laughing together like children, and took no notice of Samuel

Pollard lurking at a nearby stall. But he took notice of them.

As everyone around them packed up their wares, Pollard pre-
sented himself with gregarious courtesy, and Esther, mellowed
by her sister's company, made an effort to be polite. They made
small talk about the market, the weather, the health of each
other's friends and family members, until finally Ysabel gave
Esther a level look and declared she saw a funny-looking crow
up ahead and skipped a little distance away to give them a
chance to speak privately.

"Miss Hawthorn," said Pollard, as they strolled, "you must
know how ardently I admire you and your family. Yours is an
ancient and sacred task, but also the most modern occupation,
instrumental to the development of grammar in service to the
king. I can think of no other craft that is so nobly cross-eyed as
yours, with one eye gazing into the past, and another into the
future."

He paused, here, for Esther to express her thanks. Esther
looked ahead, and said nothing. Pollard cleared his throat and
continued.

"You must know that, as our lands lie together"—he blushed
at the metaphor—"there is a great deal we could do to develop
that practise further! Your family hasn't expanded its holdings since . . . well, since it came into them, and we've willows
aplenty on our land; only think of how much our families could
prosper, if we married and Hawthorn Willows doubled their
production—"

"They wouldn't," Esther said, firmly. "The Liss doesn't run
through your land, it runs along it for less than a quarter mile.

Do you think that if we married, your trees would
grow more enchanted?"

"Of course not," said Pollard, patiently. "But your family's name is the attraction. All willow works the same in
conducting grammar, every educated person knows that, but
the common folk will cling to their superstitions while the city
folk crave anything that comes with a stamp of rustic authentic-
ity. There's a fortune to be made, Esther, if you set aside your—
well, we are intimate enough for frankness: your selfishness.
We don't need to . . . to *incline* towards each other to be good
business partners. I think you'll find I have a very modern sen-
sibility, and won't mind if you have your dalliances, though I'd
expect that attitude to be reciprocated."

"I see," said Esther, quietly. "Have you anything more to say?"

"Please," said Pollard, reaching for her hand, "don't give me
your answer now—I know you're a young, handsome woman
and you've certain dreams and expectations of marriage as a
great romance. I can give you that, too, I promise—I've been
trying to give you that—but you must admit the practicality of
the matter. Think of what you could do for Ysabel's prospects—"

Esther snatched back her hands and slapped him, hard,
across the face.

"Speak my sister's name again," she hissed, "and I'll feed you
your tongue. Good day, Mr. Pollard."

She stalked forward to catch up with Ysabel, who kept quiet
the rest of the way home.

After dinner, the sisters went out to sing to the trees. Esther launched
into "John Barleycorn" before Ysabel could say anything—a very
charming song, beloved in the west country, which is either about

the planting, reaping, and milling of barley or about the ritual consumption of a man brutally murdered several times over. Esther sang it very much as the latter.

By the time John Barleycorn was reduced to sloshing about his nut-brown bowl, they'd reached the Professors, and she'd calmed down a little. The sisters lay down beneath the trees with their heads together as the evening chorus of small birds began around them, picking up where their own singing had stopped.

"Esther," said Ysabel, softly, "I want to ask you something, but you have to promise not to get angry."

Esther drew a long breath in, and let a long breath out. "I can't promise that. But I promise I'll try not to stay that way long."

"Fair enough. All right. Do you hate Mr. Pollard so much because he deserves it, or because he's asking to marry you while Rin isn't?"

Esther said nothing for a long time—long enough that Ysabel started to say, "You *promised*—" just as Esther finally said, "Bel," and she didn't sound angry at all, only sad, as she said, "when did you get so wise?"

"Oh, just this morning," said Ysabel, smiling, relieved. "Mama poured some wisdom into my oats."

"Well," said Esther, rolling up to sit cross-legged and pluck at some grasses, "I think it's a little of both. I truly detest Pollard—his overfamiliar way of speaking, the airs he puts on, his way of seeing the world—but you're right that it isn't really him I'm angry with. But it's not Rin, either, it's—"

"Why *not* Rin?" Ysabel pushed.

Esther frowned. "What do you mean?"

"Why not be angry with Rin! They're not treating you

seriously, Esther. I want you to be happy, I do, but—I don't like to see you always waiting for someone who only visits when the moon is right."

"They come when I call," said Esther, softly.

"Sometimes, but—they don't even want to meet your family! I know you enjoy each other's company, but they must know that your place is here. Don't they?" Ysabel looked at her sister, hopefully, then expectantly. ". . . Isn't it?"

"Of course it is, but—" Esther hesitated, then threw up her hands. "Look, why should I have to marry anyone? Why can't we just live here, like this, together, you and me, taking lovers as we like and raising children together and teaching them to sing to the trees? Why should marriage mean me leaving or someone else staying? I don't know, Bel," she said, sighing. "You're all the family I need."

"But," said Ysabel, "I'm not all the family you *want*."

Esther looked at Ysabel, stricken—looking for the reproach in it, the forked shape of their old bruise. But Ysabel just looked sad.

It hung between them. Then Ysabel sighed, sat up, draped her arms over her sister, and kissed her cheek.

"I love you," she said. "Go and find your Arcadian."

It is well known that folk journey into and out of Arcadia, just as it's well known that people travel into and out of the Levant. But it's not done *regularly,* reliably, or particularly safely; one understands that one's life is about to irrevocably change by having embarked on the journey, by the rigours of the journey itself, and by all the mysteries attendant on arrival.

There are lands that are near to us geographically but far from us temporally: London is not Londinium, though it's built from its bones. There are lands that are near to us temporally but far from us geographically: we can be certain that at this moment, in Italy, someone is sitting down to their breakfast with a newspaper dated roughly the same as ours, though we cannot expect to reach them in time to join them for the meal.

When Arcadia overlaps with the lands we know, it takes years to journey into it; when Arcadia is some distance away, it is possible to conceive of it as contemporary. It is always both at a remove and always immediate; always near to hand and very far away.

For this reason, Esther was not journeying into
Arcadia. Rin was of a people to whom time was a kind
of instrument, distance a kind of music, and while she did
not know how to play, they could meet in the Modal Lands
without too much difficulty, and did, as often as they could.

Some evenings, when Esther set foot over the boundary
of the Professors' roots, she found it morning, and the stone-
strewn gate of the Refrain quite nearby; other evenings the sky
didn't much change, but the Refrain was over the brow of a hill.
This evening was one of those, and she set out along the river,
singing as she went.

> *I gave my love a cherry that has no stone*
> *I gave my love a chicken that has no bone*
> *I gave my love a story that has no end*
> *I gave my love a country, with no borders to defend*

The Modal Lands shimmered, shifted beneath her feet; the
Refrain loomed before her.

She felt a hand in hers.

"But how," said a voice like snowmelt, cold and fresh, "can
a cherry have no stone? And how can a chicken have no bone?
How can a story have no end? And how"—Rin's long fingers
interlaced with hers, then tightened—"can a country have no
borders to defend?"

They'd stopped walking; Esther looked at Rin and smiled,
twined her other hand with Rin's and sang her riddle song's
replies:

> *A cherry when it's bloomin', it has no stone,*
> *A chicken when it's pippin', it has no bone,*

The story that I love you, it has no end,
A country in surrender, has no borders to defend

Rin closed their eyes, and bent their forehead to hers. They stood that way, holding hands and leaning towards each other like the Professors, while the Modal Lands hummed around them.

Moments like this, Esther was jealous of her own voice. She wanted to make Rin look that way with her touch, with her kisses, but only her singing produced this kind of dissolved and aching bliss in her lover. Esther didn't think her voice was anything special without Ysabel's—she had a good ear, certainly, and her voice came clear and strong, but singing without Ysabel's harmonies made her feel like a candle without a wick.

Unless Rin was listening. Then she felt like an angel, or a queen.

It always took Rin a moment to gather their wits after a song. When they lifted their head from Esther's, they raised her hands to their lips, then kissed them, slowly, carefully, precisely: the back of her hands, then her palms, then her wrists. Esther flushed, trembled.

"I missed you," she whispered, sinking down to the ground with them, as Rin pulled her close.

"Since this afternoon?" they murmured, looking at her the way she sometimes looked at sunsets, or the afternoon light winding its way through willow leaves.

"We didn't do *this* this afternoon. And anyway it's always too long." She chuckled softly. "Long as a road that has no end."

"I wondered," said Rin, pulling back to look at her with their river-jewel eyes, "about the last line, about the borders. Did you make it up?"

"It came to me on the way here," she said, lean-ing her head against their chest. "I was thinking of Arcadia, if I'm honest, but I couldn't work it into the rhyme scheme."

"Arcadia has borders," said Rin, sounding puzzled. "We're on its borders now."

"No, no—it's more complicated than that," said Esther, sitting up straighter. Rin looked amused; it pleased them to be only one of Esther's several passions, on roughly equal footing with damson jam and the patterns in riddle songs.

"There are two ways to answer these riddles," said Esther, drawing her hands back to gesture with them. "With the past, or with the future. We think of the cherry or the chicken as unchangeable things, and the song pokes at those assumptions. How is a cherry not a cherry? Well, when it's a flower. How is a chicken not a chicken? Well, when it's an egg. The song says, this thing you are used to, it has a past, and that past is part of it; what the cherry was *before* the cherry is part of the cherry. All right?"

Rin nodded solemnly. "All right."

"But that's only one set of answers," said Esther, picking up a pebble to illustrate her argument. "The answer to what was the cherry before the cherry? And that's one version of the song. But there's another version of the song, with different answers—the answers to the question, what is the cherry *after* the cherry?"

Rin lifted an eyebrow. "A second cherry?"

Esther punched them lightly on the shoulder, and they laughed. "My apologies, please go on."

Esther rolled her eyes, but smiled, and did so.

"The cherry that's baked in a pie, for instance, has no stone.

The chicken that's stewed in a pot, it has no bone. The song says, this thing you are used to, it has a future, and the future is part of it, too."

"The country after the country," said Rin, thoughtfully. "The country that's surrendered."

"Yes, exactly! And I think it's all right, as answers go. But I got there because I thought, what is a country before a country? And I thought of Arcadia. And I thought, what is a country after a country? And I thought . . . That's Arcadia too. So how can it have borders to *defend,* if it's always in the past, or always in the future? What could it defend against?"

"Perhaps," said Rin, "that is how it defends itself." Gently, they drew Esther back towards them, settled her back against their chest, and wrapped their arms around her. "By never being wholly within reach."

Esther felt something in her chest buzz, like a plucked string touched too slowly and too soon. She sighed, and nestled back against Rin. They kissed her neck.

"I would give you Arcadia," said Rin, softly. "If you'd let me."

Esther smiled, sadly, tangled her fingers in the grasses in front of her. They were blue and red and purple, the colours rippling between them. "What is a gift that comes at a cost?"

"Hopefully more than what's been lost," said Rin, reaching their fingers into her hair. Esther caught them, held them to her chest.

"Rin," she said, seriously. "Will you come home with me?"

Rin tilted their head to the side, like a bird. Esther took a deep breath.

"Come home with me. Marry me. Be known as Rin Hawthorn for as long as I'm alive."

If you've ever looked into running water at midday and been

mesmerised by the play of shadows over stones,
and how even the sound of the water running seems,
somehow, to have absorbed sunshine scattered through
lines of leaves and grasses—if you've ever stood on a moor
in the west country and watched daylight flash and vanish over
the green and granite of the land—you might have a sense of
how Rin looked as they listened to Esther, hope and anguish
rippling through and around each other on the high pale planes
of their face.

"I thought you might want children," they said, gently.

"Ysabel wants children. I want you."

"I thought you might want more than fifty years with me,"
they said, a tremble in the width of their mouth.

"I want the rest of my brief life with you," she said, "but here.
Here, where I can still sing to the willows, and help my sister
raise her children, and look after my parents as they age. Here,
where my store of memories is small but sharp, and bright. I
can't leave them for Arcadia—but for you, it would be an eye-
blink, wouldn't it? A holiday. And I'd sing to you every day,
with no distance to bridge between us."

Rin closed their eyes. "There is so much sorrow here, Esther.
There is so much cruelty in all your beautiful songs. Every one
of them is a kind of fishhook in the heart, cold and piercing.
There is so much I don't understand of your life in this world. It
is an instrument I can't play."

Esther raised her chin and looked away; her eyes brimmed.
Rin stroked her cheek to draw her gaze back towards them.

"But if you'll teach me, I'll stay." Their voice rippled. "I'll
stay with you, and meet your family, and be Rin Hawthorn if
you'll have me, for as long as you live."

Esther stared, and flung her arms around Rin, and fell to

kissing their neck while they laughed in their sad soft way that sounded like small silver bells.

"Will you come with me tonight," she said, brushing back wisps of their white hair, "and meet everyone? Tell everyone we're engaged?"

They shook their head and looked towards the Refrain, which was suddenly much closer. "Soon. I have many affairs to set in order first. But we should have a token. Did you bring me a ring?"

Esther blinked, then blushed furiously; Rin laughed. "What, you came to woo me empty-handed? Come to think of it, I'd heard your marriage customs involved a bended knee."

"Look, I gave you a cherry, a chicken, a story, and a country. I should think that's quite enough for a start!"

Rin kissed her until she laughed, too. "Here," they said, and unpinned her hair; she looked up at Rin while they ran their fingers through the long dark length of it, catching at loose strands. Then they coaxed Esther's hands towards their own hair. She undid the ribbon holding it back, and trailed her fingers through the thistledown softness of it, till they'd both caught parts of each other, and Rin fashioned two small circles from their hair.

Then Esther gasped as Rin plunged their whole hand into the waters of the River Liss.

When they drew it back, two rings glistened on their palm: signet rings with braided silver bands, and their blue gemstone faces etched with a likeness of the Professors, and the River Liss running through them.

Rin dried them thoroughly in the soft linens of their shirt before offering one to Esther; she placed it on Rin's finger, and they placed one on hers. Esther gazed at her hand, and wondered at the grammar of it—not the shift of hair to jewels, but of *woman* to *wife*, so quickly, so gently.

"Are we really doing this?" she whispered.

"I'll come find you tomorrow," said Rin, softly.

"I love you," said Esther suddenly. "I love you. Rin—I can't wait for Ysabel to meet you at last."

Rin smiled. "I look forward to it."

They kissed, and parted, and Rin walked towards the Refrain and paused at the threshold; looked back at her, and smiled, then straightened their shoulders and walked through it, and then Esther couldn't see them anymore.

She sat a while longer, then stood; she wrapped her arms around herself, and twirled, and laughed, felt lifted and happy. She wanted to sing, she wanted to rush home to tell Ysabel. She felt as if she could conjugate grammar with her joy alone, as if she could reach up, grasp the sky, and shake the darkening sheet of it into dawn.

For it was dark, now—a deep velvet dark, with a fog rising up from the water. Esther peered into the distance; the Professors were much farther off now, but she was used to that, the Modal Lands undulating, shedding their aspects like snakes. She began carefully picking her way back along the River Liss.

"That's a pretty ring, Esther," came a familiar voice—overfamiliar, unwelcome, as shocking to encounter in this place as a brick wall in the dark. "I'd have given you gold, though."

Esther stopped, but could see no one through the murk and mist.

"Mr. Pollard?" Esther squinted through the haze. "What . . . what are you doing out here?"

When she finally saw him, he was far too close. He was

wearing a long black coat, she noted, and gloves on his hands, though the weather had been mild before she set out.

"I was worried about you," he said, stiffly. "And I see I was right to be. Another wholesome woman seduced away from decency by an Antique."

Heat flooded Esther's cheeks, and her hands balled into fists at her sides. She felt the cool, unfamiliar metal of her ring, and rubbed her thumb against it to keep calm.

"Mr. Pollard," she said, standing her ground as he approached her, "I've always made my feelings about you plain."

"Oh, certainly," he said, tugging at the cuffs of his gloves. "I'm not a complete dolt; I know you don't care a fig for me. But we're very alike, you know. We're both family-minded people; we're both stubborn, persistent—"

"Stubborn!" Esther snapped. "If the one I wanted had said no to me, I'd have nursed a broken heart, not whined at them like a puppy until they petted me!"

Pollard scowled. "You'd have seen sense eventually, and we'd have made a great match, if not for outside interference."

Esther laughed like a whip striking. "Pollard, you're cracked. I don't want you, I never wanted you, I could never want you. You disgust me. If we never speak again, it will be too soon."

She made to pass him. He gripped her arm with his, and held her in place.

"Clearly," he hissed, "I know better than you what's best for our families. But you're not the only Hawthorn girl, and Ysabel, at least, isn't an elf-shot whore."

And then he pushed her into the river.

From the shore, the River Liss never looks very deep. But

the River Liss seems many things at many times, and when Esther plunged into it, she did not meet the bottom. She struggled to the surface, coughing, and felt Pollard's gloved hand on her head—heard him curse just as he shoved her beneath the water again, heard the hum of grammar around them as the leather on his hands turned to fish scales and weeds.

It is difficult to drown a person, even when you've taken them by surprise. Esther fought, fury and desperation fuelling her where oxygen failed, but she fought on too many fronts. She fought the water stealing her breath, the hands pushing her down, the grammar unravelling the order of her body.

Somehow, through the thrashing of her limbs and the rushing of water around her, she heard Pollard say, clear as glass, "Don't worry," in a whisper all the more grotesque for being sincere. "I'll take good care of Ysabel."

The ring on her finger burned. The water screamed for her. The world went dark.

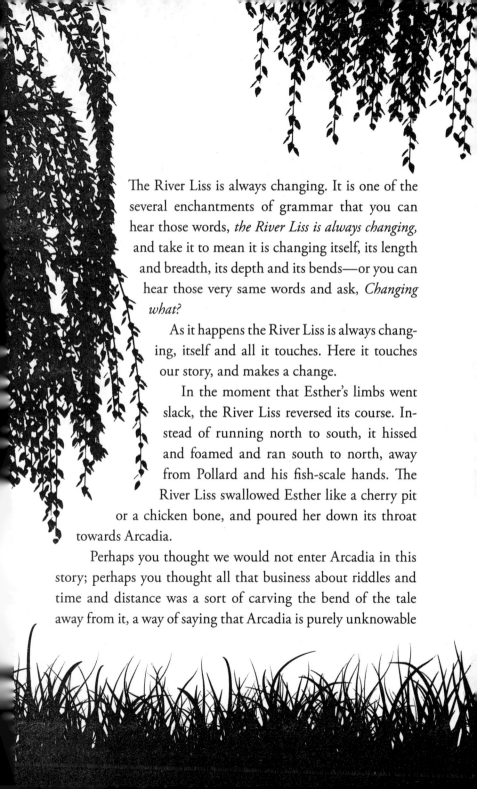

The River Liss is always changing. It is one of the several enchantments of grammar that you can hear those words, *the River Liss is always changing,* and take it to mean it is changing itself, its length and breadth, its depth and its bends—or you can hear those very same words and ask, *Changing what?*

As it happens the River Liss is always changing, itself and all it touches. Here it touches our story, and makes a change.

In the moment that Esther's limbs went slack, the River Liss reversed its course. Instead of running north to south, it hissed and foamed and ran south to north, away from Pollard and his fish-scale hands. The River Liss swallowed Esther like a cherry pit or a chicken bone, and poured her down its throat towards Arcadia.

Perhaps you thought we would not enter Arcadia in this story; perhaps you thought all that business about riddles and time and distance was a sort of carving the bend of the tale away from it, a way of saying that Arcadia is purely unknowable

to mortals, except in the case of its emigrants, like
Rin, with whom you would grow familiar through
their sojourn into our realm. You were not wholly wrong;
any part of Arcadia we glimpse in this tale becomes less
Arcadia the longer we look at it, and so in deference to our story's geopolitics, we shall not be staying long.

When Esther and Ysabel were small, seven and five, their parents hosted an assemblage of cousins, uncles, and aunts, for a May Day celebration. The kitchen bustled and heaved, children were plentifully underfoot, and there was a great deal of merrily pushing them out of doors to play games or accomplish busywork that might leave the adults some small measure of peace.

The sisters slipped away from the tumult together, given the responsibility of taking scraps to the chickens. But at the coop, one overeager hen took advantage of the girls' lack of height and experience to make her escape. The hen ran, and the girls ran after her, laughing, scolding, and so intent on their quarry that they didn't even pause at the threshold of the Professors' branches, but tumbled forward into the Modal Lands.

That day, the Modal Lands hung suspended in a golden hour's light; the seasons on either side of the willows matched, and the hills undulated softly for miles around the River Liss. But the stone arch of the Refrain had been tugged shockingly close—so close that Esther barely had a moment to frown at it before she and Ysabel were through, and only stopped, in stunned silence, when they turned to find the way behind them back to their home vanished like a shadow at noon. The landscape was all changed around them: there was a river, yes, but they could see no Professors in the dark, lichen-swept forest that sprang up all around them. Branches and stones sleeved in moss dripped moisture; the air was warm and wet.

The sisters clung to each other.

"Where are we," whispered Ysabel. Whispering felt correct—everything about this strange place seemed to demand a hushing.

"I think," said Esther, just as quietly, "we're in Arcadia." She had never seen anything quite so wholly and softly green; she reached out to touch a lacy flutter of lichen hanging from a branch.

Ysabel's eyes widened, then brimmed with tears. She had never been so far from her parents that her voice couldn't reach them. "Esther, are we lost?"

Esther looked around, at the twisting, thick-limbed trees and the dewy green light. She felt some stirring in her heart that cautioned her against answering the question; *lost* felt like a shifting, chancy word, a dangerous word to apply to oneself in Arcadia.

More than that: she understood that she needed to be brave for Ysabel.

"I'm sure we can find our way back, Bel," said Esther, firmly. "We can't be far. If we follow the river—"

"Are there wolves in Arcadia?"

Esther faltered. "I . . . I don't know . . ."

Ysabel started to cry. Esther hugged her tightly, helplessly;

she was a head taller, so Ysabel wept quiet tears into her chest while Esther held her and petted her hair and tried not to cry herself.

"It's all right Bel, it's all right," she murmured. "Let's just start walking the way we came, and I'm sure we'll be home soon."

Bel hiccupped and nodded. Then they turned around, and, holding hands, walked deeper into the forest's thick and mossy light.

Children are not reliable keepers of time, but neither is Arcadia. Who, then, can say whether the girls spent hours or minutes in that enchanted wood? To them, it felt endless—they marked the time by how long it took their clasped hands to sweat, then parted only as long as it took to dry them on their clothes before holding each other again.

But nor was Arcadia without its beauties. They saw a bird with gauzy, rainbow wings, and a tail like long, trailing fiddleheads; they saw a thorned tree in bright, fragrant bloom, hung with golden fruit. Sometimes, far in the distance, they heard the sound of horns and harps.

"Do you think they know any of our tunes?" said Esther, quietly.

"I don't *know*," said Ysabel, exasperated. "How is it so *big*? How can all this be between us and home without us knowing? I'm tired, Esther!"

She slumped down on the ground and buried her face in her knees. Esther sat down beside her.

"Do you remember," said Esther, squeezing her close, "the song about the Elven Lover? *Tell her to find me an acre of land / Between the sea and the silver sand.* Maybe that's where we are. Maybe the next step we take, we'll be home."

"Maybe," said Ysabel, glumly, looking at the bushes nearby bursting with purple berries. They knew not to eat anything in Arcadia—but they also knew they were getting hungry. Worse still—

"I'm thirsty," said Ysabel, looking at the Liss.

"Bel, no," said Esther, sharply.

"Maybe it works differently here," said Ysabel. "Maybe we could try just a tiny, tiny sip?" She scrambled to her knees and leaned over the water. Esther yanked her back.

"Don't!"

"Don't tell me what to do!"

"Children?" came a voice from behind them. "Does this belong to you?"

Esther and Ysabel shot up to their feet and turned, though Esther edged herself slightly in front of her sister, clutching her hand the while.

Before them stood an older woman (children, it should be said, are not reliable readers of age—but neither is Arcadia). She was stout and tanned, wore trousers and sturdy boots, and kept her dark hair swept untidily into a bun that glinted here and there with wisps of silver. She had a pack strapped to her back, a walking stick in one hand, and their wayward chicken nestled peacefully in the crook of her arm.

Esther was suddenly shy; her tongue stuck to the roof of her mouth. Before she could answer, Ysabel peeked out from behind her and said, "Are you a witch?"

The woman laughed—longer and more delightedly than Ysabel's words seemed to warrant, as if she'd told an excellent joke. "From the mouths of babes! Well, why not, after all. If that word keeps chasing me down perhaps it has something important to tell me." She smiled at them, and canted her head.

"It seems unlikely that you and I are going to the same place. And yet we find ourselves travelling in the same direction."

"Where are you going?" asked Ysabel, while Esther stared at her little sister and wondered where she'd put her fear.

"To a place I saw in a dream," said the woman, airily. "An old mill. It called out in a sorrowful voice for someone to bring work again to its empty body, to fill its hollow silences with the sound of water and wheels. I tired of my old employment and thought I'd journey towards it and see if the mill and I might suit each other. But I'm a ways off yet. And you, children—are you journeying into Arcadia, or out of it?"

"We . . . we came here by accident," said Esther, quietly. "We tried to follow the river back, but—"

"Ah"—the woman clucked her tongue—"an easy mistake to make. Don't follow the river. Follow the water."

Esther frowned. "What do you mean?"

"Arcadia spins you around when you enter; you can't trust your sense of direction. But there's an easy trick to it. Look." She pointed her walking stick to the river. "Which way is the current flowing?"

The girls looked. It was flowing back towards the way they'd come.

"Unless something's gone badly wrong, the water always flows *out* of Arcadia. The two of you have been travelling deeper in. I take it you want to leave?"

"We want to go home," said Ysabel, suddenly, and Esther flushed, and nodded. The woman smiled, a little sadly.

"So say we all. And where is home to you?"

"We live by the Professors," said Esther, "and came through the Refrain, near Thistleford. Our parents are—"

"Ah," said the woman, shaking her head. "Best not to speak names in this place willy-nilly. Have you eaten anything while here?"

They shook their heads.

"Good, that's simpler. Well, I'd walk you out, but it'll take me a month or so out of my way—"

"A *month*?" Esther gasped. "We can't have been gone a month—"

"Hush, child, nor have you. You're small—your names and lives sit lightly on you, and you can trip in and out of all manner of places whether you're careful or carefree. I'm on a different path, and differently burdened, and have an appointment to keep; the mill is anxious to receive me, and its heart would break if I bent my feet away from it now. But I can still help you. Listen: do you two know any songs?"

The girls nodded. If they knew nothing else, they knew that.

"Could you sing something together?"

They hesitated; then they looked at each other, and in that way they had, a knack for knowing each other's minds, they started to sing the Professors' Hymn.

The woman blinked at their voices—already, they had that grammatical shimmer to them—but turned her attention to the ground. With the tip of her walking stick she scratched marks along it. Then, as they sang, the woman lifted her walking stick above their heads, and waved it down towards the marks she'd made.

It looked for a moment as if their voices had shape and purpose, rippling in the air like a flock of starlings or a swarm of bees. Those shapes followed the sweep of the walking stick downwards, poured down into the ground, and as Esther and

Ysabel sang a path bloomed into white-gold light beneath their feet, humming softly and leading back the way the woman had come.

Esther gasped and stopped singing; as she did, the path dimmed and flickered, but did not wholly vanish. She found her place in the song again, and the path brightened.

The grammarian said, "Keep singing and follow the path; you'll soon be out. Tell your parents that Agnes Crow sends her regards, and thanks them for their work."

She set the hen down on the ground; it scratched at the song-path, pecked, then turned her back on the sisters, ruffling her feathers, and wound between Agnes' legs like a cat. Agnes chuckled. ". . . And thank them for this hen, I suppose. I hope they'll not miss her, but she has a thirst for adventure, and I think she might like to keep me company a while. Fare well, children."

Esther and Ysabel watched her go, then clasped their hands again, and sang their way out of the wood. They walked carefully, with a measured pace, to keep their voices strong and the path bright. The journey was three songs long, though they'd later argue about what else they'd sung, the time spent in Arcadia growing as mossed in their memories as the branches of those ancient trees. But the second they emerged from the Refrain, and saw the familiar bend and shape of the Professors in the distance, they bolted through the Modal Lands, burst past the trailing willow branches, and found their way home.

In later years, Esther would think back on that meeting and wish she'd asked Agnes Crow more questions when she'd had the chance: Had she been in Arcadia before? Was she a witch or not? Did she know a spell to charm chickens? Especially

because, when she and Ysabel reached home—
running, weeping, into their mother's arms—so little time had passed that their parents hadn't even noticed
they were gone.

Ysabel avoided the Modal Lands after that adventure; she
turned her face towards Thistleford and its bustling merriment,
and never ventured farther than the threshold of the Professors'
branches—where she often went to call Esther back home for
supper. For Esther went out there often, keeping her distance
from the Refrain, but observing it, wondering about it, wishing
she could talk to Agnes Crow again.

It hurt Ysabel that Esther kept wanting to go back to that
place that had so frightened them; it hurt Esther that Ysabel
wanted nothing more to do with the most interesting thing that
had ever happened to them. A year and a day after their adventure, Ysabel had been happily babbling to Esther about a troupe
of actors coming to Thistleford, and how their parents had
promised they would go and see them perform in their masks
and costumes, when she saw that Esther wasn't paying attention;
she was looking away, over her sister's shoulder, through and past
the Professors' branches as if she were listening to something
Ysabel couldn't hear.

Ysabel had started crying; Esther had, too, broken out of
her reverie and into her heart, never able to bear her sister's un-
happiness. "Bel," she said, and hugged her sister, who squirmed
against her and pushed away. "Bel, what's wrong?"

"You want to go back! You want to go back to Arcadia and
leave me!"

"Ysabel, I would *never*—Ysabel, listen to me! I would never leave you!"

She sniffled, wiping her nose and turning away. "But you want it so much."

"I—" Esther looked towards the Modal Lands. "I don't even know what I want. No, it's—more that I want . . . something I don't know. But that doesn't mean I don't want what I *do* know, and you're what I know best, Bel." She reached out to hug her again, and this time Ysabel didn't wriggle away. "You're what I love best."

Ysabel said, fiercely for all that her voice was muffled into Esther's shoulder: "Promise?"

"I promise," said Esther, and meant it with her whole heart.

In the quiet that followed, Esther felt a sudden spark in her chest, an idea kindling.

"I know," she said, pulling back from her sister to look into her eyes. "Let's make up a song together. Just for the two of us. A secret song. And if we're ever apart and we miss each other, we can sing it, and it will bring us back together."

Ysabel brightened, then looked thoughtful. "Could we still tell the Professors?"

"We'll make it up right here in front of them."

They made up their song in secret. They made it the way children sometimes make up a language to hide from adults, all invented vocabulary tacked on to borrowed syntaxes, when they know, but cannot yet explain, what grammar is. They built a song together to have their own version of the songs they were learning, and they never shared it with anyone but the willows while they both lived.

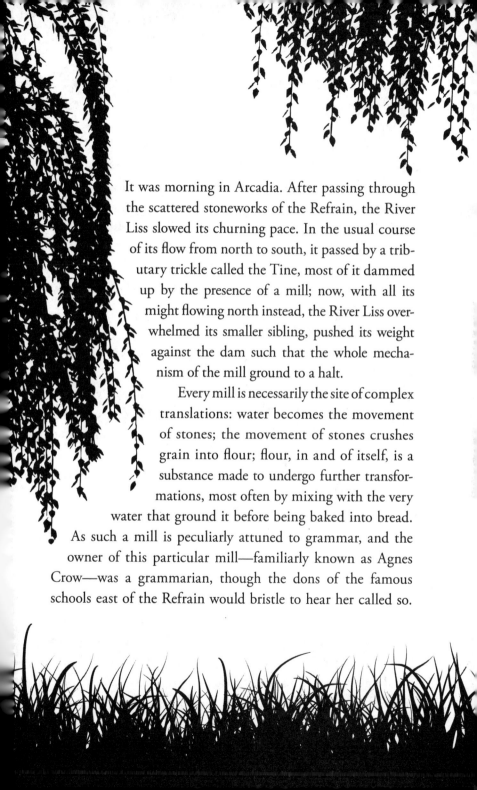

It was morning in Arcadia. After passing through the scattered stoneworks of the Refrain, the River Liss slowed its churning pace. In the usual course of its flow from north to south, it passed by a tributary trickle called the Tine, most of it dammed up by the presence of a mill; now, with all its might flowing north instead, the River Liss overwhelmed its smaller sibling, pushed its weight against the dam such that the whole mechanism of the mill ground to a halt.

Every mill is necessarily the site of complex translations: water becomes the movement of stones; the movement of stones crushes grain into flour; flour, in and of itself, is a substance made to undergo further transformations, most often by mixing with the very water that ground it before being baked into bread. As such a mill is peculiarly attuned to grammar, and the owner of this particular mill—familiarly known as Agnes Crow—was a grammarian, though the dons of the famous schools east of the Refrain would bristle to hear her called so.

She might bristle, too; she herself had a low opinion of grammarians.

At any rate, it was clear to Agnes that a powerful conjugation had taken place even before her grindstone stopped turning. She felt it as a shudder in the air, and heard it as a strangeness in the water. Imagine if you were in a room full of people speaking your most native language, but suddenly, all at once, they began speaking that language backwards; that was how it sounded to Agnes, to hear the River Liss flow north.

Agnes was shaping loaves, and had just sent her daughter out for water when the air soured; she frowned, looked out towards the millrace, and shook her head. A moment later, she heard her daughter cry out, and ran outside to find her.

"Rowan," she called out. "Rowan, what's happened, what's wrong?"

"Mother!" Rowan sounded frightened, but excited, too. "Mother, come see! There's a swan, but it's confused, it . . ." She squinted. "There's something marred about it; it has something around its neck. Oh, I hope it's all right."

Agnes stared at it, set her lips in a line, and wiped her floured hands on her apron.

"That's no swan," she said. "That's—" She stopped herself, thought quickly. "That's Rin's betrothed. Quick, we need to bring her ashore."

A swan's language is a swirl of currents, in water and air: a swan's body reads a kind of literature in the waves and clouds before launching herself between their lines. But this swan's understanding of herself and her situation was troubled, and she was frightened and angry. Why was this obstruction in her path?

Why could she not paddle against the water pushing her towards this strange object? Why did she want to lift her voice and scream when there was no one nearby to speak to, and where were her people? Why were there so many, many colours?

She lifted the long grace of her neck and flapped her wings to beat against the water. There was something on her body, something somehow both constricting and comforting, and she could not bear the contradiction—that she was trapped, and this was good, but she was also free, and this was terrible. She could not bring herself to fly.

Then a net came down, and she couldn't fly even if she'd been able to remember how. And why couldn't she remember how?

The moment that Agnes and her daughter brought the swan ashore, the River Liss seemed to sigh. It receded from the Tine; it found its southward flow again. Agnes felt the relief of it palpably in the air around them and in her own body, as if she'd been hefting a great sack of flour for longer than expected and had finally been able to set the burden of it down. Her shoulders ached with it.

"Right," she said. "Let's have a look at you."

Together they untangled the swan from the net, and Rowan wrapped her arms around the bird while Agnes peered at it. It wore a bauble around its neck: a band of braided silver with a carved blue stone in the center.

"Oh, for goodness' sake," she said.

"What is it?" said Rowan, anxious even as she tried to calm the bird.

"It's a mess, is what it is," said Agnes gruffly. "Here's a grammar lesson for you, child. Why do you suppose this woman is a swan?"

The swan stilled at that; Rowan stroked her head gently.

"She must've fallen into the Liss."

"Yes, of course, but why a swan? Why not a fish or a stone? Think back, what's the first rule of grammar?"

Rowan thought. "Every conjugation is also a translation," she recited dutifully. "But not every translation conjugates. Transformation implies movement, but things can move without being transformed."

"Yes. And so every conjugation has a logic, a pattern—a road along which to move." Agnes gestured to the swan's neck. "What's that?"

Rowan frowned. "It looks like a signet ring, only it's too big . . . oh! Signet, like . . . *cygnet,* like the name for a young swan! So it was easier for the Liss to make her a swan?"

"Indeed. The Liss saved her life with a *pun.*" Agnes looked at the swan thoughtfully. "Or a kind of riddle, I suppose. When is a signet not a signet? When it's a swan."

"Can you change her back?"

"Unlikely, without Rin's help. But," said Agnes, looking out towards the Liss, "I'm sure they'll be along shortly."

Shortly was right; moments later, clouds troubled the light. A thunderhead brewed up in the distance; the wind changed direction and turned cold, blowing in from the north, spreading frost beneath it like lace.

WHERE IS SHE, whipped a voice in the wind. *WHAT HAVE YOU DONE WITH HER, WITCH?*

"Fished her out of my millrace, if you must know," said Agnes, crossly. "Rowan's looking after her. Climb down out of your air and darkness if you want to have a conversation."

The wind howled, spun around the mill three times, then whirled down into an icy-looking Rin, a head taller than Agnes, looming over her. Their eyebrows and hair were rimed stiff; their eyes were wholly black, and their whole aspect was of a vicious blown snow, the kind of dry, cutting powder that billows in the wind like sand and cuts cold and hard against the skin of anyone unfortunate enough to be caught in it.

"Where is she?" said Rin again, more quietly, in a hiss.

"Rin," said Agnes with a sigh, reaching out to brush snow from their shoulders. "She's in a complication. You felt the river change course?"

"Everyone did. There were floods upstream."

"Well, that was for her. And for you, I imagine, for the pair of you together. I want you to come see, but I need you calm, all right? And one more thing." Agnes drew a deep breath. "I need you to not say her name."

The black twisted out of Rin's eyes as they widened, as Rin seemed both to melt and shudder into something more like a person. "No—"

"She's been marred," said Agnes, gently, "and the bond between you two is the strongest grammar we have to work with. Don't say her name until you've seen what's happened, and understand the shape of the choices before her. Is that clear?"

While Agnes spoke, Rin shrank; they no longer towered over her, but stood at a human height, and reached for her hands with theirs.

"I'm sorry," they said, "I'm sorry. I heard her cry out, but I couldn't find her, and the river was talking backwards and it was so hard to move against it—"

"I accept your apology," said Agnes, "but let's not waste any more time."

The swan became agitated as Agnes and Rin approached, till Rowan could scarcely hold her. But then she stiffened, and tucked her body behind Rowan's and her head beneath her wing.

Rin dropped to their knees in the mud. "My love," they said, in a thistledown voice, "my love, I'm here. Look at me, please."

Rowan stepped carefully away from the swan, flushing a little, to give them more privacy; Agnes had no such qualms, and watched while Rin stroked the swan's long neck until she calmed enough to look at them. Rin traced the edges of the silver band around her neck and raised their ring finger to it, leaning the blue stones gently against each other.

Meanwhile, Agnes drew a willow wand from her sleeve.

"Can you help her to find her voice, Rin?" asked Agnes. "She hasn't made a sound since we found her. Find her voice, and maybe she'll find her shape again."

Rin hesitated, but cleared their throat, and looked into their swan's warm brown eyes as they spoke, haltingly: "I gave my love a flower that had no bloom. I gave my love a bed without a bedroom. I gave my love a nettle that had no sting. I gave my love a voice that had no singing."

This was not a song by any means, and cobbled together on the spot, and if Rin's love had had her voice, she'd certainly have teased them over the lack of unity, the tuneless hodge-podge nature of it. Rin wished she would—but the swan said nothing, only blinked at them with her too-human eyes.

Rin's pale cheeks flushed with the impertinence of what they were about to ask, but they looked to Agnes. "I need to give her the tune. Have you any instruments?"

Agnes turned to Rowan, who blinked, but nodded, and ran inside. She returned with a penny-whistle, and offered it to Rin; they put it to their lips, and played the melody a few times through, before speaking, coaxing, "But how can a flower have no bloom? And how can a bed not have a bedroom? How can a nettle have no sting? And how can a voice have no singing?"

Rowan hummed the bars between verses, and Agnes, with a creaky voice worthy of her surname, joined in, while Rin covered their ears for decency's sake and struggled not to hear them; the women repeated it into the quiet, kept looping it, until the thicker, droning hum of grammar shimmered around them, and from the swan's throat came a clear, low voice:

> *Oh a flower when it's fruiting, it has no bloom,*
> *A deep riverbed, it has no bedroom,*
> *A nettle when it's linen, it has no sting*
> *A voice that's from Arcadia, it has no singing.*

The swan leaned her head on Rin's shoulder, and Rin gathered her up gently into their arms, and closed their eyes.

"Now," murmured Agnes, lifting her willow wand, "hold her, Rin, and don't let go, whatever shapes she passes through."

Rin tightened their grip, and braced. The swan became fire, then snow; the snow became lightning, then thorns. Rin held the burning, scorching, stabbing shapes of her closer and closer, winced and bled the bright, clear blood of Arcadians over her, while Agnes muttered grammar forwards and backwards, coaxing the truth of the woman back into memory and flesh.

Then, there she was—naked and nameless in the arms of her lover, save for a silver ring, but otherwise all herself.

Rowan hurried forward with a cloak to wrap her in, and was startled to hear her chuckle.

"This," she said hoarsely, leaning her head against Rin's chest while they rocked her, "has been a very strange wedding day."

Agnes smiled sadly. "I'm afraid it isn't over yet, my dear. Listen—we all know your name but won't say it, and you mustn't, either."

She frowned, wary. "Why not?"

"Because you have a choice to make now, and it will be a difficult one; and whatever you choose, your name will be the seal, the stamp that holds your chosen form in place."

The woman—who'd been through several ordeals in a very short span of time, relatively speaking—looked confused, and Agnes sighed; but she was nothing if not inclined towards good pedagogy.

"You know how, when you repeat a word over and over quickly, it loses its meaning?"

The woman nodded, carefully.

"Well," Agnes went on, "your body has been through a great deal of repetition, and the grammar holding you together has come loose. The meaning attached to your name has gone slack, and we want to tighten it up again. But," she said, and here she looked to Rin, who looked away, "that needs to be your choice."

"I don't understand," she said, though she was struggling to. "Why would I not want to remain as I am?"

Agnes sighed. "How did you come to be in the river, my dear? Can you recall?"

She frowned. The river . . . the darkness of it, the churn . . . the fog, and the black coat coming out of it, and fish-scale hands—

"Pollard!" she suddenly spat. "Samuel Pollard. He pushed me. He tried to drown me! He said— Rin, he wanted me gone so he could court my sister for our land! We have to go back now, tell everyone—"

Rin bit their lip. She saw them bite back her name, too, and felt them stroke her hair in a gesture that spoke the same wary, gentling sadness.

"Beloved," they said. "He did drown you. You died, on the other side of the Refrain. Your ring, the bond between us— that allowed the River Liss to bring you here, because part of you belongs to Arcadia. I'd hoped . . . I'd hoped you'd have to make this choice in fifty years. But it's here now. So, you can either remain here in this shape, with me, forever—or you can go back through the gate, and die as soon as you step beyond the bounds of the Refrain."

The drowned woman stared at them. She stared at her hands, her arms—paler than they had been, closer to Rin's colouring now, and with a rainbow sheen to them, like oil.

Dead. She couldn't be. Not with a sister whose children she still needed to meet. Not with parents to whom she'd not said goodbye. Not when she'd been promised, *promised* a future not hours ago, a future she craved, where her loves didn't pull her in different directions but could sit together beneath the Professors' boughs and talk of the weather and what songs to sing to the trees. Dead, and Ysabel would never know she'd meant to come back. Ysabel would think—

"That isn't *quite* right, Rin," said Agnes, carefully. "Be clear. She came here in the shape of a swan; she could live as a swan on the other side. It's your human body, my dear, that can only live here now."

"I couldn't speak, as a swan," said the woman. "That's how

you unravelled the grammar, isn't it? You helped
me sing."

Agnes nodded. The woman stood, shakily, wrapped
the cloak more tightly around her, and began, slowly, to
pace.

"So it's a riddle. When is a woman not a woman? When she's
dead. Or when she's a swan. But I need—Agnes, I need to be
able to speak. I need to be able to tell Bel what happened, to
accuse Pollard—"

Rin said, "Could I not go and tell them?"

She shook her head. "Not without some proof; he's well re-
spected, and no one knows you. And what if he accused you of
having killed me? No, I have to go."

Rin looked at her helplessly. "Perhaps you could send a
message—"

Her eyes flashed. "She's my *sister*, Rin!"

"And you," they said, as the air crackled around them, "are
my *wife*, and I don't wish to lose any more of you."

Agnes held up a hand. "Peace, please. I think," she said, looking at Rin, then turning back to her, "that Rin has forgotten
how little the rules of grammar are understood outside Arcadia.
What you're proposing implies another translation, and they
know that every translation incurs some loss."

"I'm not afraid of that. She's my sister," said the woman again,
but more quietly. "I would die for her. If I've really died . . . I
want to have died for her."

"And I," said Rin, softly, "only want you to live for me."

"Rin," she said, "I'm sorry. I want to be with you. But I was
an elder sister before I was a wife, and for longer, and that's a
shape I can't easily shake." She looked at Agnes. "I can't be alive

on the other side unless I'm a swan. But can I be dead, and have a voice?"

Agnes squinted. "That sounds like a riddle too. How would you solve it?"

The sister smiled, looking at Rin, and sang, brazenly:

Lover, tell me, lover, tell me, how do Arcadians sing?

And Rin, lifting a hand to her cheek, answered in speech. "With their flutes and their bells and their horns and their shells, and the shiver of their harp strings."

She put her hand over theirs, leaned into their touch, and closed her eyes.

"Make me into a harp," she said. "Can you do that? Make me into a harp, and call it by my name, and take me home to my sister."

Rin had no need of willow wands to do this work, and Agnes gave them their privacy. She and Rowan went back inside to shape the long-neglected loaves and set the rest of the mill in order, while Rin and their beloved walked to the banks of the River Liss.

Rin stepped into the water, fully clothed; it reached just above their knees. But when they held their hand out, she hesitated, looking from Rin to the water.

"I won't let you go," they said, gently.

"You haven't yet," she said, and took a deep breath. She dropped her cloak, and grasped Rin's hand. Their rings touched. She stepped forward, expecting to sink.

Her feet met the river bottom; Rin's hands grasped her shoulders, and together they sank to their knees, so the water reached their chests.

She kissed Rin first, deep and long, uncertain whether she ever would again. She looked into their river-jewel eyes, drew a deep breath, then turned and leaned her back against their chest.

Then Rin began to shape her into something new.

Most music is the result of some intimacy with an instrument. One wraps one's mouth around a whistle and pours one's breath into it; one all but lays one's cheek against a violin; and skin to skin is holy drummer's kiss. But a harp is played most like a lover: you learn to lean its body against your breast, find those places of deepest, stiffest tension with your hands and finger them into quivering release. You rock together, forward and back; your left hand keeps a base rhythm while your right weaves a melody through it, and they flutter past each other as the music becomes more complex, swells, breaks, shakes the body of your instrument in joy and grief alike, in the wild, wonderful grammar of being alive.

"Esther Hawthorn," said Rin, panting, raising the harp from the water. Its frame gleamed golden white, its strings were black as hair, and its column was crowned with a band of braided silver set with a carved blue jewel.

"Esther Hawthorn, sister to Ysabel; Esther Hawthorn, my wife. Will you sing for me?"

They set the harp down on a stony expanse of bank, and the wind brushed through the hair of its strings—but it needed no wind to play its song. It began to play alone, buzzing and uncertain at first, too soft to be heard—but then it lifted its voice like the neck of a swan, and the music soared, and poured out of Arcadia with the waters of the River Liss.

On the night that Esther didn't return home, Ysabel forced herself to be glad, at first. She thought, *Well* done, *Esther, embracing your Arcadian, losing track of time;* she expected to find her sister rosy-cheeked and grinning as she made her way back over the Professors' roots, and Ysabel knew just what song to chide her with. She'd sing:

> *A light dragoon came over the hill,*
> *when the moon was shining clearly*
> *There was a little lady*
> *and she knew them by the gorse*
> *because she loved them dearly.*

Then Esther would laugh and protest that there had been no gorse, and they'd sing the song to the willows anyway, and then Ysabel would glory in all the gossip of the meeting, and in seeing her sister happy.

But that was not what happened. Ysabel sang to the willows alone that morning, and that night.

The next morning her mother joined her, and held her hand, and asked if the rumours were true about Esther's Arcadian lover, and Ysabel bit her lip and would not betray the confidence, but her silence was telling enough. Then her mother sighed, and said Esther wouldn't be the first, though she'd thought better of her than to leave without saying good-bye. Once her mother turned back home, Ysabel wept into the Professors' roots, and felt herself, for the first time in her life, utterly alone.

The next day, Samuel Pollard came to visit.

He strolled with her along the willows, looking haggard and sad, though Ysabel knew he couldn't be that upset, really—he wouldn't be there if he were. He wore new leather gloves that seemed to fit him poorly, for he kept flexing his palms into fists as if wanting to stretch the material, before thrusting them into his pockets when he noticed her looking at them. Perhaps he had a cramp from writing; she'd heard gloves could be worn to help with that sort of thing.

At any rate, Pollard was kind to her, and courteous, and he spoke so sadly of Esther's leaving, and he asked her about Esther, and Ysabel found herself telling him all the many, many things he'd done wrong in trying to woo her as he had, and he laughed in a way that made her feel bolder, and say more.

"I suppose it's a comfort, really," said Pollard. "I might have felt a pricking of my pride if she'd chosen some other lad, but who among us could compete with an Arcadian?"

That silenced Ysabel, who knew that of course *she* could, that Esther, *her Esther* would never have left her—but she had, hadn't she? And hadn't Ysabel told her to go find her Arcadian? Had

Esther thought herself absolved by her sister at last, released from a child's demanding and unreasonable promise?

It all hurt too much to think about, and before she realized quite what had happened, she found she'd taken Samuel Pollard's arm. His eyes widened, and he smiled gently and leaned towards her.

"Perhaps, Miss Hawthorn," he said, briefly pulling a hand out of his pocket to pat the one she'd placed on him, "perhaps you'd be so kind as to tell me how *you* would best like to be courted?"

She turned away then, blushing, but also wrinkling her nose; something smelled unmistakably of fish.

Pollard asked Ysabel's parents for their permission to court her, as Rin never had with Esther, and they granted it with aching hearts; they could see Ysabel would benefit from the distraction. So Pollard invited himself over for tea there once a week. He knew all the latest fashions in London, and brought Ysabel mirrors, bonnets, hair ornaments, catalogues to browse; if his conversation was a little vulgar, and if he thought he knew more than Ysabel's mother and father about the properties of their willows, well, everyone had flaws. But when he took turns with her around the garden, his attention was wholly hers, and he never once looked towards the Professors or the Modal Lands.

Ysabel did, though.

One day Pollard came with a special gift. A frequent bone of contention between him and Ysabel's father was the notion that all willow wood conducted grammar the same way, and that the Hawthorns' willows, while undoubtedly expertly managed, were no better at it than any others. He decided to prove it.

He brought Ysabel a beautiful lap desk, and as she unwrapped it on the kitchen table, he explained that he'd had it enchanted in Exeter just for her. He showed her its compartments, its inkwell, its handsome feather quill.

"Now," he said, pulling out two willow wands, "this one is mine, made from good stock near London; this one is from your willows, and, I'm sure, equally good. But you'll find there's no difference between them." He picked up his wand; he muttered Latin, and waved the wand over the assembled objects.

Ysabel gasped. The quill rose from its place, dipped its tip into the inkwell, and began to write.

"Oh," said Ysabel, eyes wide, "it's *wonderful,* Sam—" She could see, and it moved her, that the quill was writing her name.

"Yes, I've been experimenting with the pastoral mode. Now," beamed Pollard, picking up the other wand, "I'll use yours, for the same task."

The quill wrote on, and Pollard smirked. "You see? It's just as I said—"

But it was writing faster, now, and harder. Ysabel winced as the paper tore. "Samuel—"

Pollard frowned, spoke Latin, shifted his hand in the air. "Hm. That's odd."

Then the quill caught fire.

The feathers burned unnaturally long, long enough for Ysabel to find a bucket of water while Pollard shrieked; the flames had caught the grease in his hair.

In a moment, Ysabel had doused them both. Pollard, sopping wet, left in a rude whirlwind of embarrassment and rage, and Ysabel bent over to clean up after him.

There was a poem on the singed and sodden page.

To Ysabel, my pretty belle,
My little love, my willow,
How great you make my heart to swell
With your longest hair of yellow.

But then, beneath it, in a different, jagged, twisting hand:

Demand better.

Ysabel crushed the paper in her fist and ran outside to the Professors.

She looked up at their long and sweeping branches, and laid a hand on the nearest trunk. She bent her forehead against it, drew a deep breath, and lifted her voice to sing.

Ysabel's voice was higher and clearer than Esther's; of the two, she was the more accomplished singer, though it hardly mattered when they performed together—their voices twining was something so much more than either of them alone.

But Ysabel, bereft, didn't sing to the Professors. She sang to Esther, their secret song, in a choked and ragged whisper.

She sang to bring her sister back to her, and she waited. But Esther didn't come stepping over the river or its roots, and in a world where grammar was real it felt deeply, unbearably cruel.

She waited until the sun set. Then she went back inside.

When Pollard appeared the next morning, bearing flowers and copious apologies, she smiled at him, and demanded nothing at all.

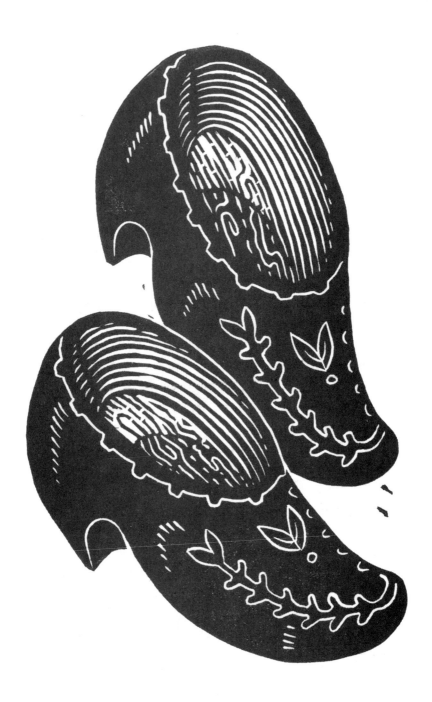

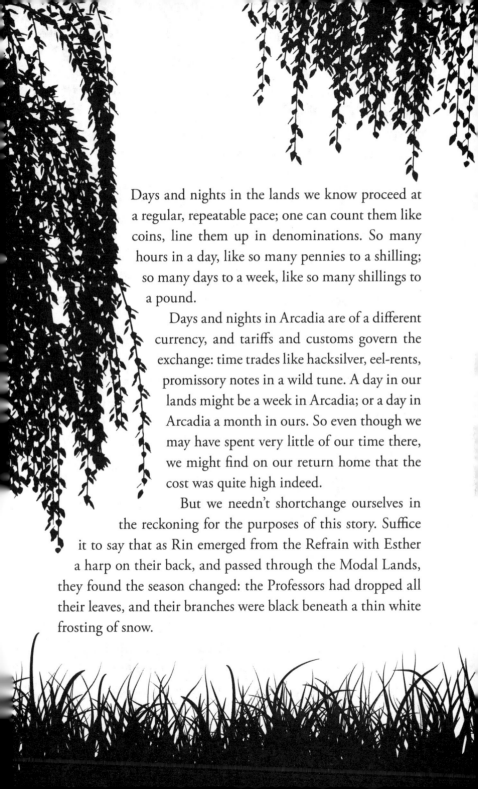

Days and nights in the lands we know proceed at a regular, repeatable pace; one can count them like coins, line them up in denominations. So many hours in a day, like so many pennies to a shilling; so many days to a week, like so many shillings to a pound.

Days and nights in Arcadia are of a different currency, and tariffs and customs govern the exchange: time trades like hacksilver, eel-rents, promissory notes in a wild tune. A day in our lands might be a week in Arcadia; or a day in Arcadia a month in ours. So even though we may have spent very little of our time there, we might find on our return home that the cost was quite high indeed.

But we needn't shortchange ourselves in the reckoning for the purposes of this story. Suffice it to say that as Rin emerged from the Refrain with Esther a harp on their back, and passed through the Modal Lands, they found the season changed: the Professors had dropped all their leaves, and their branches were black beneath a thin white frosting of snow.

When Rin and Esther arrived at Hawthorn House, they found it ringed in merriment. Everywhere were lamps, candles; everywhere were people dancing.

"A harper!" called a neighbour. "A harper, well met! Come, come, that's all we lack, we're celebrating an engagement!"

Rin was ushered inside.

They looked around the room. Everything was arranged in a circle around the hearth; there sat Ysabel Hawthorn and Samuel Pollard, she smiling wanly and he beaming expansively as folk shook his hand and congratulated the newly betrothed. Ysabel and Esther's parents sat, too, conversing with neighbours and farmhands.

There was one empty chair, hastily placed there for the harper. A hush fell on the room as Rin approached it, and as people saw the harp more clearly. It was obviously Arcadian work.

"Friend," said Ysabel's father, standing. "Have you travelled far today?"

"Half a candle's breadth I roam," said Rin, sadly, "with just enough to light me home."

The room grew colder, tensed.

Rin said, "I understand this to be a merry occasion, and that songs of celebration would be most appropriate. But I've heard it said that the young mistress of the house favours murder ballads."

Rin looked at Ysabel, who had not once looked away from the harp since they'd brought it inside. Her heart beat hard and fast enough to be an accompaniment.

Pollard frowned, but before anyone could say anything further, Rin placed the harp on the seat and stepped back.

The strings shimmered, and everyone tasted grammar on the

air like honey and salt, and a voice rose out of the instrument playing itself—low, and clear, and familiar
to everyone in the room, singing the story of her unmaking.

No one so much as breathed while she sang, until she
came to the last few verses.

> *Yonder sits my mother Eileen*
> *Hey ho and me bonny oh*
> *Who taught us to sing to the willows green*
> *The swans swim so bonny oh*
>
> *And by her sits my father, Hugh*
> *Hey ho and me bonny oh*
> *Whose love for us was dear and true*
> *The swans swim so bonny oh*
>
> *And by them sits my sweet sister Bel*
> *Hey ho and me bonny oh*
> *There's none but her I love so well*
> *The swans swim so bonny oh*
>
> *And by her sits that villain, Sam*
> *Hey ho and me bonny oh*
> *Who drowned me for the sake of my land*
> *And wears fish scales on both his hands*
> *And whose destruction I demand*
> *The swans swim so bonny oh*

The song ended. Rin's eyes were closed while Ysabel's were
wide, wide open; both their faces shimmered with tears.

Samuel Pollard staggered to his feet.

"This is obscene!" he shouted. "Some Antique frippery! How dare you, filth, come traipsing into this hall with your parlor tricks and gewgaws? More likely *you* killed her, and have come to claim her inheritance for your fairy friends!"

Everyone gasped at the obscenity. Rin said nothing, but curled their long fingers into fists and narrowed their eyes.

"Take off your gloves and show your hands," said Rin lightly, "and we can settle this as your sort prefers."

Pollard flushed, sputtered, and thrust his hands into his pockets by instinct.

Ysabel stood.

"Enough of this," she said, and the quiet of it carried as if by grammar. "Arcadians can't sing. Esther told me that." Her voice caught on the thorn of her sister's name, and tore. She swallowed around the pain and said, "Esther and I had a song we made up together when we were small. No one else knows it. It's a riddle song."

Ysabel drew a deep breath, lifted her chin, and sang.

Oh what is longer than the way?

And Esther replied,

The time from you I've spent away.

Ysabel's eyes brimmed, and she took a step closer.

Oh what is deeper than the sea?

And Esther answered from her hollow wooden heart,

The depth of my true love for thee.

On the last verse, Ysabel reached out a hand to touch the harp, as her tears spilled and their voices wove together:

Oh what is stronger than a death?
Two sisters singing with one breath.

They say voices run in families. Esther and Ysabel's voices ran together like raindrops on a windowpane, threaded through each other like the warp and weft of fine cloth, and as they harmonized, the air shimmered with grammar, and Ysabel could see her sister in the harp, whole and beautiful and unmarred, and no one who heard them could doubt that this was Esther Hawthorn, come herself to name her murderer.

That murderer ran, too. He didn't get far.

The townsfolk wanted to hang him, but Ysabel stopped them. She made an alternate proposal, and everyone agreed it was just. They made arrangements, and then marched him out to the border between his lands and the Hawthorns'. There, while he wept and begged, they forced him to drink water from the River Liss in a willow-wood cup, and Esther's strings were tense and still as she and Ysabel watched her murderer stripped of his name and shape. His legs thickened into a single smooth trunk; his arms stretched up into branches; his

screams were extinguished by a thickening of
bark over his mouth.

"It's an unruly willow," said Ysabel, quietly. "It needs
coppicing."

Wherever its branches were cut, it bled.

The next morning, Esther and Ysabel sang the Professors their
hymn. Rin watched them from the Modal Lands, then looked
away while Ysabel hugged the harp to her, weeping softly into
its neck while it played her a lullaby.

Once she'd recovered herself, Rin approached.

"I wish," they said, "that we'd met under different circum-
stances."

"So do I," said Ysabel, rubbing the heel of her hand into her
eyes. "You should have introduced yourself sooner."

Rin hesitated, but then nodded. "Yes."

"You made her so happy, you know, but I hated whenever
you visited her, because . . ." She tried to laugh, but what came
out was strangled. "I was so afraid of losing her to Arcadia! Ever
since we were small, ever since that time we fell in—the way
she looked at everything around us, I knew her heart was set
on it. Everywhere she looked she saw a whole hidden world of
riddles to solve—except when she looked at me. It was as if . . .
if it weren't for me, she would be on an adventure. But *she* was
my whole world, so I made her promise never to leave me—so
childish, so selfish!" She stroked the crown of the harp, gently.
"But she found a way to keep that promise, you see? She kept it.
She came back to me, even though she died."

"Esther," said Rin, in a voice that, for all that it was quiet,
made Ysabel think of howling winds on a lonely cliff at night.

"Would you prefer to stay? Here, as a harp, but with your family."

The harp began to play a selkie song, and sang:

Oh woe is me, oh woe is me,
I have seven bairns on land
And seven in the sea.

"No," said Ysabel, suddenly, clapping her hands on the strings to still them. "No. You kept your promise, and you're free of it. Go, be with your Arcadian. We'll be all right, Esther," she said, and smiled to make herself mean it. "I'll be all right."

Rin said nothing, but in a way that Ysabel appreciated. They looked out towards the River Liss—towards the Modal Lands, and the Refrain beyond.

"Ysabel," they said, and as they looked at her Ysabel understood, suddenly, every time Esther had struggled to describe Rin without reference to landscapes and seasons. "The promise she made to you brought her back from the dead. You might ask yourself—what promises have you made her?"

Ysabel stood, stunned, while Rin lifted the harp and slung it over their back.

"You are my sister-in-law," they said, quietly, "and the way should be easier for you. But it will still be very hard."

Rin put a hand on her shoulder, and leaned down to murmur something into her ear. Ysabel's eyes widened. Rin nodded to her, then stepped beyond the Professors' boundary with Esther on their back. Ysabel watched them go until the Modal Lands folded them away.

* * *

You'll want to know, of course, what Rin said to
Ysabel. It's only natural, and I am sympathetic. But
if I told you, you'd be in possession of a terrible secret,
wouldn't you? One that kings and grammarians alike would
kill to possess. And who are you, ultimately, to be trusted with a
way into Arcadia? Who's to say you aren't yourself a grammarian,
or a king?

Rin might have said, *The way is a riddle. How would Esther
solve it?*

They might have said, *You sang your way out of Arcadia once;
sing your way back in.*

Or Rin might have said, *If the river has roots, it has branches,
too; learn to climb them, and find your sister.*

It all returns to grammar.

There is the grammar of a sentence, which can mean an ar-
rangement of subjects and verbs, or can mean transformation
into a tree that bleeds red where it's cut. There is the grammar
of grammarians, refined and removed from its source, and the
grammar of witches, daily conjugating water into bread.

There is grammar that is ruled like a kingdom, and grammar
that is ruled like a composition book, and there is always, always the wild, unruly grammar of ballads and riddles, and this
is the grammar of Arcadia, which breaks the real into the true.

But I will tell you this much.

The River Liss runs north to south, and its waters brim with
grammar. From its secret sources in Arcadia it rushes, conjugating as it flows into the lands we think we know.

Beyond those lands, through the scattered stone gates of the
Refrain, where the River Liss meets the River Tine, a woman
with dark hair and a voice like a harp is visiting friends with

her spouse. Their friends run a mill, and share a history, and they all spend time together with a generous hand.

Esther Hawthorn, and Rin Hawthorn, and Agnes and Rowan Crow. They are about to sit together for supper, but Esther pauses; an extra place has been laid.

"We're expecting a visitor," says Agnes, with a shrug, "but expecting isn't the same as receiving."

There comes a knock at the door. Agnes says, "Esther, would you get that?"

Esther, puzzled, does.

She opens the door, and Ysabel stands there: panting, eyes wide, grinning like she's won a prize. She no longer looks like the younger sister—Arcadia has smoothed over the gap in years between them. On her feet are willow-wood clogs; on her shoulders is a small child, sucking a thumb, gazing at Esther with Ysabel's own bright eyes.

"We're here to remind you of the words to 'Tam Lin,'" she says.

And their joy runs together like rivers, like voices, like families.

Turn the page for a sneak peek
at Amal El-Mohtar's upcoming
short story collection.

JOHN HOLLOWBACK AND THE WITCH

The witch had no name that he knew. John Hollowback found her house at the far end of a fallow field, browning with the fall: a small cottage of wattle and daub, with a thatched roof and a smoking chimney, nestled up against a forest of birch, poplar, and pine. He could see a well nearby, a tidy garden, and a store of seasoned wood stacked against the eastern wall.

It was a pretty place. He thought perhaps he was mistaken; it did not look like the home of a witch. Still, he walked to the door and knocked three times.

The woman who answered was most certainly a witch.

Her hair was dark, greasy, wisped in grey and falling messily out of a loose topknot; her skin was sun-browned and crinkled around her eyes, which were a strange, flashing blue. She did not look very old, but was hideous enough to be recognisable as one who practised magic.

"What do you want?" Her voice was low, but clear.

"I want a whole back, instead of a hole in my back," he said, firmly.

She squinted at him, and gestured for him to turn around, poking at him curiously while he did.

Though he walked without a stoop or limp, John had a hollow in his back. Where spine and sinew were meant to make a bold line from neck to tailbone, they vanished instead into an oval cavity the size of a serving plate, lined with pale, soft skin.

"I used to be called John Turner," he said, bitterly. "Now folk call me Hollowback, like an old tree. Owls could nest in me."

She placed her hands against his shoulder blades, knocking against them like a door. She rapped her knuckles down his back until they met wood and the sound rang out hollow indeed. He winced.

"I made myself a board to cover the hole. I daren't be alone with women—"

"You're alone with me," she observed.

"You know what I mean. I have seen doctors, and they can do nothing. Can you help?"

She pulled her hands back, folded her arms, and considered him.

"Perhaps," she said. "Come in."

She led him towards the hearth and sat him down; he turned his back to her, lifted his shirt, and unfastened the leather bracers holding a thin sheet of wood against his hollow like a lid. He shivered as she felt around its edges, hissed when her fingers brushed the tender flesh within.

"I see," she murmured. "I see. You're missing a pound of flesh. Who did you cross?"

His shoulders slumped beneath her hands. "No one. I have no debts, and some money put by. A year ago I was to propose to my love; a year and a day ago I woke with a hollow in my back, and this frightened her away, and she never spoke to me again."

"Mm." She withdrew her hands. "A pity—it is difficult to restore that which has been taken by another."

"Then you cannot help me?"

"I did not say that." She tapped a thoughtful rhythm against his back. "But it will take some time. You will have to stay here for the duration. What have you brought with you?"

He lifted the flap of his bag and pulled out a leather-bound book.

"I thought you might value this, and take it as payment," he said, offering it to her. She raised a thick eyebrow, picked it up, and thumbed through it.

"It's blank," she said, looking at him curiously.

"It's magic," he said, "I think. Anything I try to write in it vanishes. I have no use for it, but I thought, perhaps, someone with your craft—"

"What else have you brought," she said, snapping it shut and tossing it aside. John flushed, swallowed, and poured out the rest of his bag.

He had packed sensibly: a change of clothing, some food, some money, along with his tools. But from among his belongings the witch singled out an apple, a comb, and a bit of string. John blinked; he had not packed them.

"These," she said, "will be of some use. Tomorrow we'll begin tending to your back. You are a woodworker, I see?"

John nodded.

"I will take my payment in trade, then. Go to sleep."

The witch sat in her garden while John slept, puffing a pipe. He didn't remember her; that much was clear. What he *did* remember remained to be seen.

She clicked her tongue in the language of bats until one swooped merrily around her head; she whispered with it a while, then watched as the bat wheeled away into the velvet dark.

John woke to the witch shaking him gruffly by the shoulder.

"We begin today," she said. "You'll do chores while it's light; at night, we will work together on your back. Is this fair by you?"

"Yes," he said, sitting up, "yes, of course."

"Good. You must understand that once we begin this process, it will be difficult to stop. It is as if you are carrying a knife stuck in your back; if I pull it out, a dangerous gushing will result, and if you do not let me complete my work, it will go badly for you. I say this because it will be painful, and I will not hurt you without your consent. Do you understand?"

John felt suddenly unsure. "It will hurt?"

"Most likely. Great changes often do."

"Only, I don't remember it hurting when it happened."

The witch only stared at him, waiting.

John chewed his lip, then nodded. "And I only need to do chores? You don't want the book, or . . . a promise, of . . ." He swallowed what might be an insulting assumption. ". . . some future thing?"

The witch looked more pitying than contemptuous. She reached up to clap him on the shoulder.

"John Hollowback," she said, "you have absolutely nothing I could possibly want."

On that first day, John swept the witch's floors, scoured her pots, drew water from her well, and scouted a space outdoors to set up a spring-pole lathe. She'd said she expected trade, but nothing else; he wanted to be prepared. By the time the witch called him in, he had most of it done, and had worked up an honest sweat; she'd set out a robust dinner for the two of them, bread and cheese and a thick vegetable stew. They ate in silence—not quite companionable, but not awkward, either.

Once they'd finished, John cleared the table and washed up; the witch, meanwhile, set the apple on the table, and waited for him to join her.

"Take off your shirt," she said, "and your board, and lie down on your belly."

He did as he was told, if reluctantly; it was not easy to show his naked back. He found he was less ashamed about it with the witch, though; perhaps because she wore her own ugliness so brazenly, he didn't so much mind his own. Wherever he came face-to-face with people they found him handsome: he was after all tall, with straight teeth and a small nose, high cheekbones and honeyed hair. But when he turned his back, he knew people shuddered at the shape of him, whispered about the odd way his shirt hung off his shoulders, a strange sag at his belt.

He propped his chin up on his folded arms and gazed into the dimming embers of the fire while the witch moved around behind him.

"I'm going to make a scrying bowl of your hollow," she said, "by painting it black, and filling it with water. While I do this, I want you to tell me the story of this apple."

She held it out to him. He frowned.

"It's just an apple. I must've packed it for a snack and forgotten about it."

"It spoke to me," she said, simply, "from among your things. You seem to be missing more than flesh, John Hollowback—there are memories you carry outside your body, and I don't think you'll be whole again until you've recalled them." She sat down next to him on a low stool, swirling a paintbrush through a pungent stone jar, and began applying its contents to his back.

He hissed—it was cold—then wrinkled his nose, annoyed. "That's nonsense. I'll grant I don't remember my hollowing, but I've a decent memory in general, and—"

"Eat it."

He blinked. "What?"

"Eat the apple. Take a bite."

He was rather full from dinner, but he shrugged his shoulders, parted his lips, lifted it to his mouth—and stopped, suddenly wracked with nausea. He gasped, sick-drool pooling around his tongue, and turned away from it, panting—but could not drop it, though he felt it growing warm in his hand, echoing something thumping hard in his chest.

"You can't eat it," said the witch, her voice rougher than he would have liked, "any more than you can eat your arm. But you can tell me the story of it." She laid another long, thick line down the bowl of his back while he caught his breath.

John turned the apple over in his hands. It was, he thought, a lovely specimen, red and round, its stem flying a single leaf like a flag; it looked just-picked, carried the scent of the orchard with it, the fizzy smell of ferment rising up from fruit crushed underfoot. Nothing in his bag had broken or bruised its surface; he owned as that was odd. But a story? The story of the apple was that it was a mystery, though the more he looked at it, the more he cupped it in his hands, the more he felt an unaccountable tenderness welling up in him.

He flinched as the witch poured a pitcher of cool water into his back, exhaled as she stirred her finger through it.

"I see," she murmured, "a great many trees, and among them a wagon, brightly coloured. There are women picking apples, but the wagon—"

"Oh!" said John, suddenly. "Of course, yes—that was when I first met her. Lydia, my—" He grimaced. "She was working, bringing in the fruit, and she was singing . . ."

The witch said nothing, but slowed her stirring. John found himself tugging at the thread of memory—perhaps this was what she meant, by telling the story? The apple reminded him of something, and he shared it? He groped his way to a better beginning.

"I was travelling with a troupe of players—not a player myself, of course, but I'd make their sets, mend the boards they trod, and they gave me a share of the take. William and Janet, they were married, and Brigid, she wasn't their daughter but may as well have been. We travelled in a caravan that was both advertisement and stage—or, well, they all did, being a family. I usually followed after them on a mule, stopping in towns to ply my own trade and sleep in a bed before catching them up at the next stop—more comfortable for everyone that way, the wagon was only so big.

"Well, we were setting up in this orchard with the farmer's permission, and this girl was up a ladder—she was fine enough to look at, but her voice was something else. She was singing, leading the other workers in a song, call and response, and it was like hearing a lark among crows. I stopped setting up, stopped everything just to listen to her. And when the song was done I strode up to her and said as how I'd loved her singing, and her voice was a gift, and why was she picking fruit when she could be travelling the country and sharing out the gold of her music? And she blushed and smiled and plucked an apple from a branch near her cheek and held it out to me, and said that was very kind, but she was only a country lass. But we got to talking, and I brought the players out to meet her, and she watched our show. And that did it. She was off with us the next morning."

The water in his back felt warm now, not unpleasantly.

"Give me the apple, John," said the witch, quietly; she coaxed it from his hand—he found it hard to release—and then rolled it around the edge of his hollow. A ringing rose in his ears, a pain, a sharp slicing of grief—and then water sloshed over the edge of his hollow and he cried out, spun quickly to face her, scuttling back and away on his palms and making a mess of the floor.

The witch looked at him coolly.

"There. That's one." She looked from him to the puddle on the floor, and stood up slowly. "Enough for now, I think. Mop that up. Don't bother putting your board on tomorrow—it won't fit. Best give your back a little room to breathe."

She walked out to the garden, leaving John gasping, reaching around to touch the familiar contours of his hollow—and finding, instead, an inch more solid back than he'd had before.

The next morning, John woke late; the witch had let him sleep in. He was glad of it: he felt sore and stiff throughout his body, as if he'd spent a long night drinking. He stretched, and scratched, and reached cautiously towards his hollow. His shoulders slumped in relief when he found his new flesh still in place. He looked around for a mirror, and saw one hanging on the wall; steeling himself against the possibility that it might do him some mischief, he approached it and tried to catch a glimpse of his back in it.

The hollow was certainly smaller—but a thin black ring marked its previous circumference. He frowned. Perhaps it would fade in time.

He could hear the witch puttering out in the garden, and dragged himself to the bread and cheese she'd left on the table— next to the leather-bound book she'd refused from him as payment. Or had she accepted it? She was an odd one—she spoke plainly, but John felt there was much she didn't say.

As he munched his breakfast, he decided there was no harm in opening the book.

Then he choked.

The first few pages had writing on them. Not just any writing; the story he'd told the witch last night.

Well, he thought, that made sense; who better than a witch to write in a magic book? Perhaps that had always been its purpose—to be a witch's grimoire, inscribed with spells.

Funny that she'd write his own story in it. Odd, too, to see his story laid out by another, in writing. It seemed, at a glance, much longer than his own telling.

He skimmed over the memory of apples, and felt, again, the pang of losing Lydia, the sting of betrayal, the anger and shame of it. There had been so much promise at first, and then, at the end, no hint of anything amiss until she was gone.

"Good, you're awake," said the witch, standing in the doorway, tugging off her gardening gloves. John startled, slammed the book shut, and turned to her equal parts furtive, guilty, and defiant.

She did not seem to notice. "The day's getting away from us. Do you need me to make you a list, or can you get on all right just looking around at what needs doing?"

She made him a list, in the end, and once he'd chopped

wood and hauled water to her satisfaction, he turned back to finishing his lathe.

He thought he might make the witch a bowl, as a small joke, since she'd made one of him. He found a likely birch log, split it in half, and began chipping out a rough shape. He'd just gotten as far as fitting it onto the lathe when the witch came out to see him, and he noticed the hour gone late and golden around him.

The witch looked at the lathe with frank curiosity. "I see you've not been idle."

John's hollow back straightened somewhat. He took pride in his work.

She stepped around to his side. "Would you show me? Or is it a trade secret?"

John demonstrated the mechanism—how the treadle tugged the pole down and spun the wood to be shaped in one direction, then the other as it released. "You only cut on the downstroke," he said, "slowly, carefully. Then it springs back up—it's called reciprocating action—and you push down again, until it takes the shape you want."

"Fascinating," she said, quietly. "Very clever. Does the wood ever break, or crack?"

"Not if it's sufficiently green, seen to by a steady hand."

"I see," she said. "And is this light enough to work by?"

"No," he admitted. "I should leave off for tonight."

"Wise. And so shall I—I don't think you're entirely recovered from yesterday. Come and have something to eat."

That evening, their meal together was more genial; the witch asked about his back, whether he'd felt any pain after their ritual.

"No," he said, "but there's a black ring . . ."

She shrugged. "Sutures leave scars. It's all part of the process. I can't undo what happened to you; I can only help mend it."

She asked, then, about his memories of travelling on the road.

It had been a bright and venturesome time; they'd performed in villages and taverns, but also led the occasional masque or revelry in a grand country hall. Their summers they spent on the road; in winter they sought the shelter of familiar fields, farmers and sometimes gentry glad of the entertainment during long, cold nights.

It was while holed up together that they came to know each other best, he and Lydia. Her arrival had expanded the group's repertoire: where before they'd performed scraps of entertaining miscellanies, told stories, made use of John's modest skills in puppetry, now they had a full complement of players—though it meant Brigid usually took on trouser roles to play a young lover opposite Lydia's ingenue, or else a puckish troublemaker needling William and Janet's grumpier elder roles.

But Lydia was indisputably the star.

"Did you never perform with them?" asked the witch, pouring them both a fragrant tea after they'd eaten.

"I did before—if they needed someone to be a prop, or a mark, or to move a puppet. I'm no actor, I know that—hard not to when you travel with those who have the gift. But once they had Lydia, it was better to keep to making and mending. She cast a long shadow."

"Were you jealous?" she asked, with a frankness that felt like a slap.

"No," he said, staring at her. She held his gaze. Eventually he looked away. "No. But Brigid was."

The witch chuckled, and John frowned. But she stood and asked him to tidy up after their meal, putting an end to the matter, then walked out into the garden. He was asleep before she returned.

The next morning John woke early, but not earlier than the witch, and found a bowl of porridge laid out for him as well as some late plums. The leather-bound book was there, too.

He watched it while he ate. He looked out towards the garden, where the witch likely was.

He pulled the book towards him, opened it, and read.

Lydia picked apples and sang as she worked; she loved hearing her voice strong and high, feeling her call pull in a chorus of responses, as if she cast a net to catch her fellows' breath. But when she stopped, she felt eyes on her, and turned to see a tall, thin young man staring.

"That's a terrible ladder," he said. "It's dangerous, you could fall. Let me fix it."

Lydia laughed, for the ladder had borne her weight without wobbling all season, but she hopped down and let him have his way. As he shook his head and set about tightening the rungs, he said, "You have the most beautiful voice I've ever heard. And I've heard plenty. I'm John, what's your name?"

"Lydia," she said, smiling. "Thank you, that's kind."

"No, it's just true."

She asked if he was with the caravan of players, and he said he was. Her eyes shone, and she said she was looking forward to the show, that she loved the music and stories; he paused in his work, and said he could take her to meet the players, if she wanted.

She did want, very much.

She met William, Janet, and Brigid in short order; John intro-

duced her as the voice of the orchard, and she rolled her eyes, but said she did love to sing. Brigid's eyes caught hers, and she asked about her favourite songs, and they fell to talking like they'd known each other for years but had not seen each other for more, familiar and starved for each other, while William and Janet exchanged fond looks and John sat silent and looked at everyone apart from himself.

John tasted copper before realizing he'd bitten through his lip. He shut the book, then opened it, fingers trembling. Then he shut it again.

How dare the witch? He'd come to her with his hollow, his history, and she had made of it—whatever this was, a fanciful embroidery, some kind of cruel taunt.

Had he even said he fixed the ladder? He recalled, now, that he'd tightened the rungs, but it hadn't seemed worth mentioning. Was that really the first thing he'd said to Lydia?

He shoved his porridge aside and stormed out to the lathe.

The work soon soothed him. His world narrowed in focus to angles and pressure and speed, the beauty of wood smoothed and shaped, every rough part sheared off into a tangle of delicate blonde curls. By the time the witch came out to find him, the finished bowl gleamed.

"Here," said John, stiffly. "Trade."

The witch raised her eyebrows at him, and took the proffered bowl, turning it in her hands. "It's lovely. Well done."

John flushed, but looked away. The witch eyed him, then said, lightly, "I know just what to do with it. Come with me."

He followed her into her garden, where she wandered, stooped, cut lettuces and herbs with a short sharp knife. Whatever she cut, she placed in the bowl, until it was heaped with brilliant, tender greenery.

"Walk with me, John," she said. "We'll not be long."

"Where are we going?"

"To visit a neighbour. Now, what's the matter?"

He scowled. "Nothing."

"It's the wrong season for lemons," she said, "but you look like you've been feasting on little else. And you didn't clean up after breakfast; that porridge'll be crusted to its bowl like a barnacle."

He rolled his eyes. "Pardon me for having made you a better one."

The witch stopped walking, and looked up at him. Her eyes flashed—literally, magically—and he looked away, fuming.

"John Hollowback," she said, calmly, "you'll keep a civil tongue in your head when you speak to me, or else you'll keep a home in your back for owls. Is that understood?"

He chewed his lip. "Yes."

"We made a bargain, and I have asked very little of you. Tell me what's wrong or keep your own council, but do not think to insult me or my crockery with your backhanded foolishness while accepting my hospitality. Shame on you."

She walked on, and reluctantly, he followed.

Eventually they came to a cottage, and were warmly received by the couple inside: a woman, heavily pregnant, her husband beaming solicitously alongside her.

"I brought these for the cravings," said the witch, pressing the bowl into the woman's hands. "Make a salad of them, they'll be good for you." She looked to John, and smiled. "John here made the bowl."

John stood awkwardly by while the couple gushed their thanks; they pressed a small loaf and a jar of bramble jam on them, which the witch handed John to carry. Mercifully she declined their offer of dinner. They began their walk back in silence.

"I made that bowl for you," said John, who wanted to be angry, but was mostly tired. The witch shrugged.

"And I traded it for bread and jam. I did say I'd take my payment in trade." She looked at him, levelly. "And that I wanted nothing from you. I always mean what I say, John."

"I thought," said John, who wanted to be vicious, but wasn't up to the task, "that witches hated giving up their greens. That they punished people for taking from their gardens. We did a whole show about it once."

She chuckled. "And why not? Everyone wants to see a witch punish someone for stealing from her. A witch is a kind of justice in the world. It makes for a fine story. No one wants to admit the truth, for all it stares them plainly in the face."

"What's that?"

"Steal from a woman long enough, and a witch is what she'll become."

They'd reached the cottage. John drew a deep breath.

"I'm sorry," he said, grudgingly, "for being rude. But I saw what you'd written in the book, and I didn't like it."

He didn't like, either, the pitying way the witch looked at him now.

"John," she said, "I've not written anything in that book."

* * *

She laid him down shirtless in front of the hearth again, painted another layer of black into his hollow. She handed him the comb, poured water into the bowl of him, and propped the leather-bound book open to a fresh page where he could see it.

"I believe I understand," she said, "what has happened to you, and the way it came about. But it's a little like trying to rebuild a tree from a pile of wood shavings. There is so much you don't remember, and it's necessary that you do. So: tell me the story of the comb."

She began stirring the water in his back again.

John looked at the comb: it was very elegant, long-handled and decorated with flowering vines carved out of the wood. He recognized his own work.

"I made this for her," he said. "I made her lots of things—but I could say they were for the troupe, if I were building scenery that would show her particularly well, or making improvements to the wagon. But I made her this as a gift, from me to only her, and she let me brush her hair with it, and I knew then that she loved me, to let me stand so close to her."

The water in his back heated up much more quickly this time, and less comfortably. He shifted on his belly, and looked from the comb in his hands to the open book in front of him.

It was filling with writing. He squinted to read it.

John prided himself on introducing people to each other. He was no great performer, but he liked to say that he was the trusses that held up the stage, that he carried them all on his back. Sometimes he would ride ahead of the wagon and make connections through his woodworking—connections which he then leveraged into perfor-

mance opportunities—and sometimes he would hang back after the show to glean gossip and carry that back to the group. He had an uncanny knack for placing himself between people, and resented the existence of any closeness that did not widen to admit him.

He resented Janet and William's direction; he resented Brigid and Lydia's friendship; he resented Lydia's passion for performing, and the audience's passion for her. And the more he resented them, the more he plied them with gifts, words and wood and wooing coated in the venom of his need.

John hissed. The water in his back steamed. "It's not true," he gasped, "it's not true."

"Tell me what is, then," said the witch quietly, stirring the while.

"I loved them." His lip trembled. "I loved them all."

But he looked back to the book, and read.

To William and Janet, he brought a pair of beautifully turned bowls, and while they ate together he spoke grave rumours of unfriendly villages ahead, dislike of outsiders, a dwindling of prospects leading to a hard winter.

"Some say it's unnatural for women to play men on the stage," he said, his eyes soft and sad, *"and mutter dark things to each other. Honestly, I fear for Brigid—but I'm sure these words will pass like weather, it's probably nothing."*

And William and Janet paled, and reached for each other's hands.

To Brigid, he brought hand-carved dice, and played games 'til they were deep in their cups, and spoke of Lydia's talent, her brilliance.

"But I worry," he said, "that she'll only ever be thought of as one half of a pair—that she'll be stamped like a coin into one role until she's spent."

And Brigid frowned, and John looked contrite, and said, "It's not that I think you're smothering her," and paused, "but I do think she feels smothered."

And Brigid looked stricken, and the next morning went with a pounding head to have a word with William and Janet, and was soon visiting nearby family for a spell while Lydia's heart shook to see her go.

To Lydia, he brought a hand-carved comb, beautifully wrought with flowers and vines, and offered to dress her hair before she mounted the stage, as Brigid used to do.

"You know," he said, combing her long, bright hair, "when you stand on stage you shine."

She smiled softly. "Thank you, John."

"But sometimes," he said, "you shine so bright that it hurts to look at you. You're like a small sun, and lesser stars can't be seen when you're out."

Lydia's throat hurt. "Does it bother you?"

"No, no, of course not." He paused. "But I think it bothers Brigid."

And Brigid put distance between them, and Lydia dimmed herself, until soon they couldn't see each other at all.

And so John made room for himself.

John hardly felt the witch take the comb from him, stunned by the words and the gulf they opened in his chest. But when she began running it along the outside of his hollow, he screamed: it burned, as if the comb's teeth seared grooves around his bowlback's rim. The water that spilled over the edges of him scalded; he panted, then drew his knees in close to his chest and wept while the witch watched.

"That's two," she said, low and gruff, and left him.

The next morning, John woke to voices in the garden. The witch—and one other. He tried to rise—and groaned, his body a patchwork of pains and aches, then groaned more deeply as he remembered the source of it all.

The visitor sounded agitated, but he couldn't make out the words. The witch's voice came clear.

"I'm sorry, but I'm busy now. Come back tonight, and we'll speak more of it then."

She came in a moment later, looked at him, then busied herself in brewing a pot of mint tea while he found his way to a seat.

He stared into nothing while she poured him a cup.

"What must you think of me," he whispered, "to hear me say what I do, and then read what's written in that book?"

The witch shrugged. She poured herself some tea and sat down. "What do you think of yourself?"

"I hate it," he said. "I don't recognize the man in those pages. It isn't how I remember it."

"But you didn't remember any of it, at first," she said, lifting her cup, sniffing it. "All you remembered was losing your lover."

John kept silent. He blew gently on his tea.

"I don't want to wait until tonight," he said, finally. "I'd like to get it over with. Can we do this by daylight?"

The witch sipped her tea as she looked at him. It struck him, suddenly, that she wasn't ugly at all—he couldn't remember how he'd thought that.

"We can. But it will hurt you terribly."

He looked into his cup, and nodded. "I know."

Laid out on his belly again while the witch painted his back, he twirled the string this way and that between his thumbs and forefingers.

"I used this," he said, his voice a shallow croak, "to measure her finger for a ring. I wanted to make her a wooden one—I was going to ask her to marry me. But then everything went wrong."

"How? What happened?"

John's throat worked, but he couldn't remember. He shook his head. "She was gone when I woke. They all were."

The witch stirred the waters in his back—smaller and smaller circles, he felt, as his flesh had filled in, though he could take no joy in it—and said, "I see a great hall done up with harvest revelry: sheafs of wheat, garlands of asters, great rounds of braided bread."

"Yes," said John, "the troupe's last performance. William and Janet had decided . . . they'd"—he drew a deep breath— "they'd lost their taste for travel, and the take wasn't what it used to be. There was no better time to ask Lydia to marry me—I'd look after her, and we could be our own troupe together, if she wanted. I could set up shop in a town, she could sing in a proper theatre—I would've built her one from the ground up, I knew enough of the right people. I had something to offer her, and she had nothing to lose—"

"Because you'd taken everything from her?"

John gritted his teeth. "I never *took* anything from anyone. I had nothing, I came from nothing, I built everything I had for myself. I never forced anyone to do anything they didn't want to. I only ever tried to help."

He glared up at the book, daring it to contradict him. For a moment, nothing appeared.

Then black ink bloomed from the blank pages and sank John's heart to his stomach.

The night of the final performance, Brigid brought her mother to see the show, and to meet John and Lydia, of whom she'd heard much spoken. John was genial and spoke expansively, praised everyone but himself; Lydia smiled, demure, said little.

Brigid's mother looked at them together: how John's arm wrapped too tightly around Lydia whenever anyone else was around—how she wilted near him—how, if ever his gaze went elsewhere, if he were called away, she seemed to relax, to straighten, to smile more easily and speak more freely.

She looked, too, at her own daughter: how she floated away from the friend she would not cease praising in her visits home, but orbited her like a moth near a lantern.

She saw that some sick magic was at work.

"Lydia," she said, "would you lend me this fine fellow of yours? John, I noticed some odd carvings under the seats here, I wondered if you could tell me about them."

And John, flattered, turned his back on Brigid and Lydia, whose eyes found each other, and whose hands soon followed, and who, haltingly and in a daze, remembered how to speak.

* * *

Tears brimmed in John's eyes and he knuckled them away as he turned his face from the book. "You can't hold me responsible for them drifting apart!"

The witch stirred his waters placidly. "Who are you talking to, John?"

"Look, if they'd really loved each other, nothing I said or did could have changed that. I only wanted them to love me, too, as I loved them!"

"How did you love them, then?"

"They were everything to me," he said, fiercely. "They were my life, all of them together, and I was just—a tool. A handyman. I wanted to be everything to at least one person."

"Reciprocating action," she said. "Isn't that what you called it? Your work with the lathe. You'd pull her to you, and cut away what you didn't like, and then if she bounced away she was less—until you caught her again, and cut and carved until she fit in the palm of your hand."

"*I* discovered her! *I* made her a star!"

"What happened with the string, John?"

"I don't know! The performance went well—Lydia was more dazzling than she'd been in ages, she was pressed on all sides afterwards by admirers, and I couldn't find her for hours. But we were all going to sleep together in the hall that night, after the show, so I just waited. I waited a long time into the night, and when she came in it was her and Brigid together, and I couldn't . . . I didn't want to interrupt, so I pretended to be asleep until they were. And then I got up, and—"

He gasped as the water in his back began to boil. The witch pulled her finger back a second before it burned, shook the heat out. "Go on, John."

"I crept closer—I tried to tie the string around her finger without her waking, but—she did, and—"

"What are you doing?" she hissed, snatching her hand from his, looking at the string in horror. "What's this?"

"Nothing—nothing, go back to sleep—"

"Is this a spell?" She tugged at the string on her finger, in a panic, in a rage, as Brigid stirred beside her. "Is this how you—what are you doing to me?"

"Lydia, please," he said, finding his way to one knee, looking at her, his eyes large and beseeching as a dog's, "I wanted to ask you to marry—"

The string around her finger glowed like metal in a forge, then snapped and sizzled away to nothing. Lydia herself began to glow, as if stars melted into her veins, and rose up from her blankets, rose further still, until she floated above him, her hair high and wild as the lightning, and the air around her crackled with power.

"Liar," she hissed, and the word burned bright as her hair. "Liar! You've tried to cut me and bind me like wheat all this time!" And she spoke back at him every truth she'd untwisted from his words, every piece of her he'd taken while seeming to give her gifts, every day he'd ruined with his sad jealous eyes reproaching her for hurting him with her happiness.

And as John watched a witch being born, he felt a great gouging at his back, as if a giant hand in one single stroke had sheared spine and flesh and blood and skin from him, and out from the coring of his body tumbled an apple, a comb, a piece of string, and a book, and he fell down among them in a swoon.

When he woke up, it was midday, and the hall was empty. He

picked up the objects around him without seeing them, put them in
a bag, and carried them with him for a year and a day.

He screamed his throat raw as the witch rolled the string into
his hollow. The water turned to vapour; the thick paint on his
back smoked and peeled. Bones jutted beneath his blackened
skin like mountain peaks, twisted like serpents coiling, cracked
and rumbled like a thundering sky—but settled, finally, solid
and sound as good joinery. He panted and sobbed while the
witch rubbed circles along his newly filled back—whole now,
but for a small gap an inch wide and a few inches deep, sur-
rounded by three black rings.

"Good, John," she whispered. "Well done."

John slept the day through. As the hour grew long and blue,
the witch sat in her garden with her pipe, waiting for her visitor.

"I can't believe," came a voice bitter and hot, "that you would
help him. After everything he did to us."

"Sit, Lydia," she said, gesturing to another stool. "How was
your journey? How's Brigid?"

Lydia narrowed her eyes. "She told me not to murder you.
How could you?"

The witch shrugged. "He came to my door and asked for help."

"And that's it, then? He's whole now, and anyone who looks
at him will see just another smiling charming man and not
know to shun him? It wasn't for you to fix him!"

The witch raised an eyebrow. "Did you want the task?"

"Of course not."

"Or Brigid, or who, then? Be honest, now."

Lydia's eyes flashed—literally, magically. "I didn't want him fixed at all. He doesn't deserve it."

"Ah, there we come to it. And that's why I did it." The witch held her gaze. "For you to carry less of it. For him to carry more of it."

Lydia's face twisted in disgust, and she shook her head. But she sat down, and stared out into the darkness.

"I'll never forget what you said that night," she said, her voice full of burrs. "*A witch is a kind of justice in the world.* And here you are, undoing it."

The witch tapped the ash from her pipe.

"When you came into your power," she said, "what he'd done to you came back to him fourfold. But that was the end of your story with him. You began a new one; so too should he, with the remembrance of all he did written into his body."

"Why tell me, though? You must have known I'd hate it."

"I wasn't asking permission. But I thought you should know." She pinched herbs from a pouch and packed them into her pipe. "I wasn't going to let him become a secret I kept from you."

Lydia breathed deeply, and exhaled slowly. "I won't see him, or speak to him. Not ever again."

"Nor should you."

"You don't want me to?"

"No. I'd put seven seas between you first." She tilted her head towards the cottage door, listening. "In fact, you'd best be away; I hear him stirring. Give my love to Brigid."

Lydia looked towards the cottage door. Then she hugged the witch to her, kissed her cheek, and said, "I will."

She left. The witch went back inside.

* * *

John was awake and waiting for her—still pale and shaken from the pain, but calm. She crouched down next to him, took his temperature with her wrist against his brow.

"You're Brigid's mother," he said, quietly. "I didn't remember you."

"Hard to remember a witch," she said, amiably, "at the best of times."

"You knew who I was from the beginning."

"I did."

"And you helped me?"

She shrugged. "You asked for help. I'm not sure you're happier now than when you came, though, are you?"

He chuckled bleakly. "No."

"Then perhaps all I did was enjoy seeing you punished."

"May I stay?" His eyes were wide and soft. "I'll keep helping, I could make you chairs and spoons—"

"Absolutely not." The witch's gaze was sharp, and he flinched from it. "You're good at your craft, John. But people aren't blocks of wood for you to turn to your liking, and you've not quite learned that yet, in your bones." She stood, and walked over to the leather-bound book that lay closed now. "Have you tried writing in it since coming here? It might keep your words now, if you choose them carefully."

She found him ink and a quill. He sat with it a while, reading through every word, feeling his memories shift and spike and settle like the objects in his back.

He tried writing "Lydia," and it wouldn't stay. He tried writing "I wish," and it wouldn't stay, the ink swallowed by the page like a pebble by a pond.

He wrote, "I'm sorry," and the words stared back at him like eyes, and stayed.

He closed the book.

"I'm ready," he said, and handed it to the witch. She took it, turned him around, and angled the book carefully at what remained of his hollow.

It slid into place like an ending.

ACKNOWLEDGMENTS

This is going to get long, but in fairness this book is quite short, so I hope, if you're the sort of person to read acknowledgments, that you'll read it all the way to the end.

This story, like its heroine, went through multiple transformations before finding its final form. It would not have found that shape without the deep and early insights of my husband, Stu West, and my dear friends Sam Kabo Ashwell and Caitlyn Paxson. To be read with care and attention and clarity is such a generous gift, and I wish every writer such kind and exacting fellows.

I owe an enormous debt of gratitude to Hope Mirrlees for writing *Lud-in-the-Mist,* and to Terri Windling for introducing me to the stannary town of Chagford, its many wise and wonderful inhabitants, and Dartmoor more broadly. So much of *The River Has Roots* is a love letter to that enchanted place. I'm grateful, too, to Loreena McKennitt's "The Bonny Swans" for first introducing me to the ballad type of the "Cruel Sister," and to Emily Portman's "Two Sisters," for finally stirring up the itch in my soul to the point where it had to be scratched. Greater thanks than I can articulate are due to the El-Funoun Palestinian Popular Dance Troupe for their 2014 album *Zajel* and the transmission and preservation through it of "Tarweedeh Shmaali," or "Lover's Hymn," which provided the inspiration for the Professors' Hymn.

This book wouldn't exist without the tireless work of my agent, DongWon Song, whose guidance and friendship I'm daily grateful for; my editor, Ali Fisher, and her assistant editor, Dianna Vega, whose enthusiasm, encouragement, and support for this project have been invaluable. Huge thanks to Faceout Studio for the staggeringly gorgeous cover, and to Kathleen Neeley for the stunning interior art that just knocks me flat every time I see it.

I'm so honoured to have had such tremendous skill bent to the task of illustrating my work. Heartfelt thanks to Jocelyn Bright and Saraciea J. Fennell for their heroic efforts in publicizing this book and creating tour opportunities, and to Michael Dudding and Samantha Friedlander for everything they've done to market it. Enormous thanks are due to all the people who laboured to make this book a beautiful object for you to hold or an enchanting experience for you to listen to. On the print side, jacket designer Esther Kim, production and managing editor Lauren Hougen, production manager Steven Bucsok, and publishers William Hinton, Claire Eddy, and Devi Pillai; on the audio side, producer Steve Wagner and everyone at Macmillan Audio, who were all such a dream to work with and so receptive to my tentative thoughts and ideas.

Across the pond, I'm so grateful to Anne Perry for bringing my tiny corner of Arcadia into hers, and to Ella Patel, Alex Haywood, Gaby Puleston-Vaudrey, Tania Wilde, Keith Bambury, and Matthew Everett for everything they've done to manage and publicize this project.

This book is focused on sisters, but my love for my family is a river constantly running through me: my parents, Oussama and Leila, and my brothers, Jihad and Ghaith, have always cheered and supported my work no matter what, and the gratitude I feel for them and the fact of our togetherness is boundless.

Finally, I dedicated this book to two women whose rivers have fed my own roots, and I want to tell you about them.

Hoda Nassim was my music teacher. She taught me to play the harp when I was a starry-eyed fifteen-year-old obsessed with Loreena McKennitt and the desire to be a travelling bard. At a time when it would have been easy to let me ride the aesthetics of a charismatic instrument, Hoda really pushed me; grounded my whimsy in solid technique; and encouraged me to perform, to attend concerts, and to learn and play music outside of my comfort zone (folk songs in a minor key). Because of her I somehow managed to play a corrente by Handel on a lever harp. (If you know, you know.)

Hoda passed away in 2021, while I was just beginning to outline this story that I hoped to share with her. Her passing taught me things about grief that it is everyone's portion to learn in time, if you're going to love anyone at all: how a street in your city will be haunted by your memories of walking it to visit her; how finding unexpected scraps of her handwriting in your music books will make it impossible to play your instrument for a year, as you wish you'd made more of an effort to see her before her decline.

I miss her deeply. She was an incredible teacher, warm and funny and kind. She taught me as much about pedagogy as she did about playing music. I wish I could have shared this book with her, but in the absence of being able to do that, I'm sharing these small parts of her with you.

My sister, Dounya, is impossible for me to talk about in any coherent way. To say I love her is stupid and insufficient. To say I love her more than my own life reads like hyperbole instead of simple fact. This book is, if not entirely about how much I love her, then close enough for folk music.

The part of this story where Esther and Ysabel chase a chicken into Arcadia is autobiographical. When I was seven and my sister was five, we were living in Lebanon, and our mother took us to visit friends in a village called Kfarmishki. We chased a chicken past the boundaries of our friends' neighbours' yard, and soon found ourselves lost; a village is a small place, but we were smaller, and we'd never been there before. All of a sudden nothing looked familiar, and we had no idea how to get back to the lands and people we knew.

It is impossible for me to think of my childhood in Lebanon without thinking of the children there now; the children murdered, displaced, orphaned, trapped. It is impossible not to think of the children my parents were when they lived there; the children my grandparents were. It is impossible not to reflect, and to try to make you, dear reader, understand, that every generation of my family in living memory has been shaped or defined by imperial war.

As I write this, Israel is carpet-bombing Lebanon in an expansion of its yearlong genocidal campaign in Gaza. Canada and the US are callously failing to evacuate their own citizens from Lebanon, leaving them to endure bombardment perpetrated with weapons they've sold to Israel, or whose sale they've facilitated. Right-wing talk show hosts are claiming that Israel can't be invading Lebanon because Lebanon isn't a country, echoing the decades of Zionist rhetoric that "there is no such thing as a Palestinian"—rhetoric that claims the millions of people indigenous to the region, the thousands slaughtered and the millions displaced, are insubstantial, ephemeral. It's not wholly unlike seeing people talk about Faerie.

I wrote and revised this book under the mental duress of seeing horrific war crimes against my people denied, excused, laundered, in the same language I use to tell stories. I couldn't have borne this without the support of true friends and the grace of new fellowships emerging from a shared urgency in confronting that horror. To every person who has had the courage and conviction to say Free Palestine, to speak, scream, write, march, write to their representatives, confront injustice, and work for the liberation of all people: thank you. It's so hard to feel like these acts make any difference in the vastness of the world, but I am here to tell you that they made a difference to me.

ABOUT THE AUTHOR

AMAL EL-MOHTAR is a Hugo Award–winning author of science fiction, fantasy, poetry, and criticism, and the coauthor of the *New York Times* bestseller *This Is How You Lose the Time War*, written with Max Gladstone, which has been translated into more than ten languages. Her reviews and articles have appeared in *The New York Times* and on NPR Books. She lives in Ottawa, Canada.